JANE GARDAM
The Pangs of Love

AN ABACUS BOOK

First published in Great Britain by Hamish Hamilton Ltd 1983
Published in Abacus by Sphere Books 1984
1st reprint 1991

Printed and bound in Great Britain by
Cox & Wyman Ltd, Reading

ISBN 0 349 11404 8

Sphere Books Ltd
A Division of
Macdonald & Co (Publishers) Ltd
Orbit House
1 New Fetter Lane
London EC4A 1AR
A member of Maxwell Macmillan Pergamon Publishing Corporation

Contents

*This book is for Christopher and
Deb Sinclair-Stevenson*

The First Adam

My woman's made of paper. She's spread on the bed. She's figures and drawings. She's called The Tender, and she's not my wife. She's not young, neither – she's knocking on.

She's my mistress, this one. My tender mistress. Wife's at home in Welwyn and this sweaty midnight, whilst I'm sitting on the hotel bed, looking across at the other one, with the whisky on the floor and a mosquito pissing around and God knows how at seven floors up and netted windows – this moment, damp evening, Moira's waking to the Welwyn thrushes and a cold dawn.

She's lying under the Danish goose-down duvet and waiting for the Teasmade. Dead centre she's lying in our Heal's kingsize, dead centre on the winter side of the mattress. Alone.

Faithful? Yes she is. God knows why she is or why I'm sure she is. She's past fifty, mind, and men never meant that much to her. I never meant that much to her. I meant more I'd say as time wore on and I was abroad more. She likes being on her own. Less mess. Can take her time washing chair covers. Doesn't have to cook. Less washing up. And plan! How she plans. She's planned the Extension two years – ever since we came home together from KL with all the cane furniture. 'All that beautiful cane furniture,' she says, 'still in the roof. Crying out for that Extension. Can't you build that Extension now you've retired?'

'Can't afford extensions now I've retired.'

Digging in the garden. Mending stuff. Round the supermarket with her to help lift out the boxes. 'Not that loaf. You know we don't have that loaf, Bull. Put it back.' I put it back. Other old buggers trailing round likewise. Giving a hand. Retired. Other wives marching ahead like Moira. Rat-trap wives. Holding the reins. Holding the purse.

Well, there was pruning the roses.

And the decorating.

Walking the dog last thing round the block. Always the same walk. Your feet flap flap in front of you and you remember running, moving fast on your toes and dancing, long since – well, not that long since. I danced on the runway job at Heraklion.

Only sixty.

Christ, when the telex came, I said yes. 'Reply immediate,' it said. I replied immediate, 'Accept'. I accepted two years in Drab, for godsake. Back again in Drab, sorting out a mess and getting out a new tender. Back at the old Drab Intercon. Sixty? What's sixty? Heart? What's heart? That was two years back in KL. Bad, leaving KL. Bad moment. When you've worked out East thirty years there's limits to Welwyn.

Different for her. She never came out a lot. KL was the last, and she was only there three months and she never liked it. Not a woman for places, Moira. Things for Moira – cane furniture, carpets, lamps made out of animals' skins. There was Hong Kong one year – twittering on about jade. There was Kuching. Not much to be got in Kuching. Kuching nearly bust us apart and she was only there three weeks. Maybe better if it had bust us. She never got over Kuching.

'Well, it's a man's world,' she says in Welwyn. 'Bull's in a man's world out there. I'm just intruding. Construction work – well, it's not for women. Oh no – Bull's not lonely. Not the lonely type. "Do whatever you like," I say, "so long as you don't tell me." It's what we all say – all the wives. The English wives – I'm sure I can't speak for the French or American. The Japanese wives of course, they don't think about men once they've got a husband. He meets his old cronies, don't you, Bull? Wherever he goes. Best of everything. Best hotels when he's not working on site. Car and driver. Do this, do that. All expenses. And the pay's good –

not the pension unless you've thought ahead – and that's not Bull – but the pay's very comfortable and Bull's not extravagant. He loves his work. Never bored. Well, half of them, it's all they ever talk about, work. On and on, late at night, in one of their bedrooms like as not. I've seen them at it. It stops you going to bed. Well, you get bored watching them. I'd sooner be home – a woman – and have everything nice when he gets back.'

She doesn't even face – not even in dreams if she dreams – the possibility of a lack of her, a need for her. She turned away her thoughts a long time ago from what needing is. She doesn't need me any more.

She's right about the work, though. It's what I need most. They don't know what you're on about in England – work – but it's true. There's a number of us. It's not booze that's vital, or girls. No night-life to speak of, not in Drab at any rate. Not for my lot, and there's plenty like us up and down the world. Up-country work. Getting buildings up in a swamp. Getting plant out to a desert. Getting pylons fixed. Digging through a cliff. Scooping out a reservoir. Keeping the work-force sweet. Just about the only power the bloody country's kept since the Empire – big, overseas construction work. Like the British Army used to be but a bloody sight more useful. You're looking to a constructive conclusion. Years ahead you have to look, and you can see them stretched before you – satisfying. There on the bed – the figures, difficulties, options, all laid out. My willing mistress. 'Construction work'. They think nothing of engineers at home – think of wireless mechanics or something. Yet it's work where you see the world change. You see something that'll be there when we're all dead, up and finished. You see something completed – wipe your hands on a rag, nod and go away, knowing it'll outlive you. I saw Plover Cove, Hong Kong, right through, start to finish – the cove become the lake and all the villages rebuilt better on the hills and the people still putting little dishes of food out around it, to appease the dragons. I saw through the Singapore land reclamation – planes flying off a runway scarcely months ago was water. I worked with the Eyties on Abu

Simbil and saw the great old faces of the kings moved up the slope. The Eyties thought nothing of them – wouldn't cross the road to look at them, they said – carrying on about the Pantheon. 'I'd have a shot at moving that Pantheon,' I said and they screamed.

It's a club. Same folks turning up year in, year out – black, white, yellow – makes no difference. They're mates. Internationals. Intercontinentals. Always the Intercon. Hotels. They're our level – not a suite, of course: a good double room, private bath, couple of beds, one for work and one for Bull. Papers – my tender mistress – first things seen when you open your eyes in the morning and last thing when you close them at night. Wake – stretch for drawings, like Moira for the Teasmade and the Today Programme on the BBC. Well, I'm clear of the Today Programme, anyway.

I'm not unhappy.

No kids, mind.

Though maybe that's a blessing, when you look round. There's engineers I've known never seen their kids two, three, five years. Then kids get sent out for holidays and don't know their fathers. There was Abbott, walking jaunty – embarrassed – through the Olde English restaurant at the Shangri La somewhere (Jakarta?) with a bird all paint and legs. 'Nice work, Abbott,' say I. He says, 'Meet my daughter.' What sort of sense is that?

You get to act set ways. You take set parts. You're one feller to the World Bank crowd, another feller to the UN lot, another to the legal buffs, another for the oil men. You have your set jokes for nights out. Keep a supply – nucleus – for new acquaintances. Best is the Intercon. joke – goes down anywhere.

'Who is the happiest man?'

'The happiest man is the man with the Japanese wife, the Chinese cook, the English house and the American income.'

'So okay – who is the unhappiest man?'

'The unhappiest man is the man with the American wife, the English cook, the Japanese house and the Chinese income.'

You swop the nations about a bit, depending on the

company, but it's a winner most parties. Only trouble is it's been around a bit now. It's knocking on. Like my tender mistress.

She's an airport, this mistress, and she's a demon. A year or so ago she looked a treat, but she's gone down lately – literally down for it turns out she's based on mud. The big jumbos would have disappeared in her. Then we found she had, in addition, a heart of stone – and her heart, as is sometimes the way with mistresses – was not in the right place. Now neither mud nor stone need spell amen to a runway, but there was a particular set of circs. in this one that meant that they might.

So we got round that.

Then there was the typhoon. That swept most of the bitch away and we put her back again, piece by piece.

Then we had the cholera and that very nearly killed her, and it did kill a lot of men whose faces I don't forget that easy. In Singapore, Hong Kong, if there's a couple of cases of cholera, it's headline news. In Drab it's a couple of lines at the foot of the back page if there's two hundred, and no mention on the television. Just as nobody bothers to mention the malaria down the Old City. And I'd not rule out smallpox, whatever they say.

Then we had the murder. Drunken Scottish clerk-of-works shot a Sikh who'd taken his woman. Well, it was the Sikh's wife. Everything stopped then. My mistress stayed spread on the bed. In a coma. We're still just beginning to ease her out of it. This week the trucks started coming back – slow. There's men on the job again – clumps here, clumps there. Quiet still. No singing. But working again. And it's one hundred degrees.

You can't swear and threaten too much at one hundred degrees.

I never swear and threaten anyhow. Tend instead to watch and walk quiet. Being on the site dawn to dark does better than threats and temper. They see you coming, see you standing, see you camping out there all night often as not. See you not noticing heat, not noticing cholera, not scared of Ferguson blowing the Sikh's head off – so drunk

you'd never think he'd hold a gun, let alone aim it; let a man
– me – take it out of his hand like a baby. Put him to bed –
get police, ambulance. You get through and beyond fear,
through and beyond surprise, through and beyond heat.

Now and then, mind, there's a flutter in the old loins. Like
today – Sunday – here at the hotel. We're suddenly off the
site, not working – not because it's Sunday this being a
Muslim country – but because some bugger delivers the
wrong stuff. No plant arriving. Blinding, beating silence.
Men sleeping rolled in rags and sacks like parcels. In the
gravel heap – the factory they call it – where they hit the big
stones with the smaller stones and then the smaller stones
with smaller stones and the smaller stones with smaller –
and so on, for the cement. Some of them had dug holes for
themselves in the gravel, crawled in like mites in cheese. A
few lay about on top, like dead birds. A few still worked,
tapping slow, under umbrellas. They were dotted in the grey
shale like currants in a pudding. Living skeletons. Nothing
moved.

> *'In Bengal*
> *To work at all*
> *Is seldom if ever done'*

– nor yet in Drab.

They'll do this sudden, men. Anywhere out East. Just as
they'll go mad, sudden, too. Like Penang, that calm, warm
Monday with the rain falling and they all began to throw
bricks off the Ong skyscraper down on the Minister of
Works on a state visit.

I couldn't manage that one. It was Chinese/Malay trouble
and there's no Englishman equal to that. There's degrees of
foreignness you'll never fathom – like the way in Bengal the
husbands and wives shave the pubic hair off each other
every Thursday night. Off each other! Then it's Holy Friday
and they sit and itch. Then Saturday it's Bingo! It's as good a
story for the restaurants as the one about the happiest man,
but by God, it's when you feel foreign.

That day – the warm, rainy day of the fight at the Ong
Tower – I left the lot of them to it and went off to the

Botanical Gardens and watched the orang-outang they've got there hanging like a sweet-chestnut in its cage. Dying. It was dying, the orang-outang. It was a present from the President of Korea or somewhere to the King of Malaysia. He'd given them two, but the woman orang-outang had died already. This feller left – it just hung there. By one hand. Its eyes bloody lonely. Malays no bloody good with animals. I stood there half the day looking at its tired little red eyes. 'Not a bugger to talk to,' I said. 'You've not got a bugger to talk to,' and it just looked back. Then it gave a great swing, away and up, and sat looking up into the trees, across towards the Straits, north towards the jungles where it was born. Like Adam. The first Adam. It didn't throw things down on me. It sat quiet. Not that interested. It mourned. It observed me and thought, 'This is where you feel foreign.'

So – today, no work, and I get into my bathing trunks and out into the Intercontinental Hotel gardens. They bring me a blue mattress for my slatted long-chair and there I lie on the green lawns among the mallow bushes, purple and white flowers on the same bush – and God, the beautiful smell of them. There's great mountains of sweating bodies take the magic off, mind. All around. Bodies almost as big as mine. Australians, airline pilots resting. The size with them's just food and flab. Me – I'm hard as iron. Neck two foot round, growing low out of the shoulders. Thrusting. Hence, Bull.

Lie there.

Watch roses high above swinging from cement pergola above swimming pool and crows sitting in among them, looking down. When a lad comes out dressed in baby blue, hips like a girl, with coffee tray, you see crows glitter.

They flap down like floating black newspapers. They sit by you. All round you. They move up and take the sugar, or page of your paper, or coffee spoon. Sharp, evil beaks. Like grey candle grease.

But the sun's hot, the sky's blue, the roses red and – hullo. Loping over the grass with two waiters running behind there's this woman six feet tall with bangles round her ankle and arms and in a shouting-pink jellaba, kaftan, whatever.

Stalking high-heeled. Looking nowhere. Points at long-chair beside mine and waiters lay out blue mattress. Bow again. Coffee? She pays no attention. They depart. Crows watch. Even crows fall silent.

You almost close your eyes. Slide eye-balls sideways under lids as with one sweep off comes jellaba and she collapses gentle along mattress in pink bikini – green bangles, blue bangles, pink bikini, huge smoked glasses like a skull. Her stomach's not what it was. Droops a bit. Flat breasted but lean as a crane – the machine on the site, not the bird. She's bloody tanned – narrow boned. Proud. Face pretty terrible – mingy, disappointed. Like a hen.

But the face you needn't look at. She's got legs all right. Well, fairly all right. The more you look the less you see is all right. It's just the general impression. Big glamour. She's European. Or American. And alone.

She brings out letter and she reads and reads it. She folds it up and then lies back. Then she opens it again. And reads it. Two short deep lines appear above the glasses and below the line of the scraped back bleach of hair. She is in a trance with the letter.

He's left her. Or he isn't coming to find her. Or he's not been in to Cartier lately.

So the end of it is she's in my room after dinner, me on my bed and her on the chair and the tender mistress spread out with both of us looking at her.

'You mean you live with these? All the time? With these papers?'

'All day. All night.'

'You are alone?'

'There's the men. The management. The Intercon. lot. We all come and go. We meet up all the time – the world over.'

She looks around. I suppose the room has got fairly squalid while I'm on and off the site. The room-service knows my ways. Knows what they haven't to touch. Drawers have got left half open. Clothes about. Inside-out socks. Laundry list still on the floor. Tipped-over photograph of Moira on dressing table.

'Your wife?'

'A long time ago.'

'You have been married long?'

'Thirty years.'

'Thirty years. To the same woman?'

'Yes.'

A sigh. She goes to the window.

'Whisky?'

I have to get new bottle from back of my sweat-shirts and dislodge old tea-making machine. It's a cable with two wires sticking out like adder's tongue at one end, and metal ring the other. Bought it Kowloon, years back. You fix it in the shaving plug marked shavers only. Once fused the whole of the Doha Hilton and nearly killed myself, but I was young then. Get out my box of Brook Bond tea bags – Moira sends them out from Safeways. 'Maybe tea?'

She sighs again. Turns. She's a great shape. Like Katherine Hepburn. But God – the moment goes.

I remember her in the garden – the way she got them to put her mattress next to mine. Remember the letter – how old it looked. The folds were dirty. At dinner downstairs tonight I saw the poor old hands below the blue bangles and the neck inside the swathes of necklaces patched brown with maps of Asia.

No tenderness here. No more tenderness than in the waitresses – all saris and buttocks and insolent stares. Why should she be? She's knocked about. And she could be sixty. Well – sixty's nothing.

But not tonight.

So, it's a drink only and I take her out and leave her at the lift and then I go down the stairs and walk in the hotel gardens in the hot night. The crows'll still be up there watching. If I took off my watch and swung it, they'd swoop. If I listen, they will speak. 'Keep off her, Bull. There's no future. She's lost. She's one of the wanderers. She'll be there some form the next place. You've the Extension to build.'

Letter from Moira as I pass desk. Forgot to ask before. Tap letter first one corner, then another on desk. Looking down. So easy – 'Anything further, Mr Bull? Can we get you anything?' asks the Bell Captain. So easy. Just push dollars over. Ask for her room number.

She'll be in bed now, staring at ceiling, tired eyes deep in fragile bones of thin face. Earrings, bangles, rings lie on bedside table. Dry skin washed clean of paint is creased with years.

It is not kind or tender in me to leave her alone.

I insult her, standing here, not asking for her room number – old Bull, fit as a bull, except for the occasional twinge in the rib-cage. Poor old Bull, holding the corner of his wife's letter. How many years left? Ten? Not likely twenty. Nor for her neither, her with the bangles. It is Bull's duty to tap on her door.

But, here is Bull on his bed, looking across at his tender mistress, thinking that if he had any sense he would go through some of the preliminary tarmac figures and the War Clause before sleep. Here's knock on door and in come Bob and Kassim. Just as well she's not still here. Would have put up 'do not disturb' I guess.

'Now then – you're late, Bob. Thought you'd both not be coming.'

'Thought maybe if we'd any sense, Bull, we'd go over the preliminary tarmac figures. And look at the War Clause.'

'You've got a bloody mosquito in here, Bull.'

'They do no harm. We're immune. We're old.'

'Don't see where it came from. Seven floors up. They don't breed here. The water's too dirty.'

'Like us. Whisky?'

'Tea if we're doing the figures.'

Bull fills three tea cups with cold water and attaches wires to shaving plug.

'You'll blow us all sky high one day, Bull.'

'You've been glad of it often enough, Kass. Decent free cup of tea.'

'You've a letter there unopened.'

'It'll keep till we've done the figures.'

*

So we gather round the far bed, the bed of the mistress, one on each side of her and one at her feet. We touch and pat her, moving pieces of her about. Gradually we grow interested. We put down our tea-cups on the floor and as people sleep and wake around the spinning world we scrutinise this creature with gratitude, with love.

The Easter Lilies

Miss White, who was a dotty little woman with a queer, grinning glare and had long ago taught kindergarten at a good school, came back from Malta full of the lilies.

'They grow everywhere. Like weeds. At the roadsides in clumps. All among the stones,' she said.

She was talking at the church lunch.

Mrs Wellington, a warden's widow munched.

'They would,' she said. 'Why not? They are weeds in other countries. In Australia they are called pig lilies.'

'But they're free. They just grow anywhere. Beautiful.'

'I know.'

Mrs Wellington's husband had been RN, stationed on Malta in the great days. They had had a house between Marsa and Siggiewi among orange and lemon trees, a paved courtyard where they had held cocktail parties, with fairy lights and dance music on a gramophone. Three adoring, barefoot Maltese maids had looked after her and there had been a full time gardener. The lilies round the courtyard had had to be hacked. '*Hacked* away,' said Mrs Wellington. 'To make room for the roses.'

'But think of Easter,' said Miss White.

'Easter?'

'The Easter lilies. Didn't they have Easter lilies in Maltese churches?'

Mrs Wellington looked into space for a moment, or rather she looked across the church hall at other champing women in brave feathery hats who were consuming rolls and pâté and a single glass of claret – a pre-Lent treat. This was a progressive church. 'There were lilies,' she said, 'in the

Anglican cathedral. But they were not the pig lilies. They were gigantic, waxy things, like swirled up flags. Several hundred of them we had up in the chancel. Sheaves of them, specially grown. They were – d'you know I suddenly remember – they were a penny each.'

'And the wild lilies were free?'

'We never picked the wild lilies. Weeds. Of course they were free.'

'But they are lovely. They're as good as the Easter lilies here. Just a bit smaller. And we give fifty pence each here, just for one.'

The bowl in fact was coming round the tables for the Easter lily money. A bowl had come round earlier for the luncheon expenses. The lunch cost fifty pence too. Now the second bowl approached.

'Lily money,' said the Sunday School teacher bearing it, rosy faced and good.

The coins clonked on to the felt bottom of the bowl. When she reached Miss White, however, there was a pause. Mrs Wellington dropped her money in – there were a lot of half p's. Mrs Wellington kept half p's in a jam jar in the kitchen since the Captain died. They were for this sort of occasion. She brought them all to church in an envelope and showered them in. The bowl then hovered beside Miss White and Miss White peered down at it for quite a time and then said, 'No. No. I think not, dear.'

It was a surprise. A surprise to the Sunday School teacher and a greater one to Mrs Wellington. She knew that Miss White was poor but she was notoriously generous. In the seventy-odd years she had been a member of this church she – or her family, now all dead – could never once have failed to pay for an Easter lily.

'Is anything wrong?' asked Mrs Wellington.

Miss White said, 'Yes. It is ridiculous.'

'Ridiculous! At Easter?' (The Church was High.)

'The roof is coming in. The Hall is leaking. Father Banks couldn't live if he didn't eat Irish stew round half the parish four times a week, poor soul. And we spend fifty pence each on Easter lilies. I shall get some from Malta.' She gave her dotty grin, the grin which at school they had all imitated in the cloakrooms. In the breathy, high voice that had not changed in all the years and which they had also imitated, in the playground and even in front of her if she had come out to clap her hands for quiet (and she had never minded and they had always obeyed), she said, 'I'll write to Malta and get some sent.'

*

In the pink, tipsy-looking house built under the walls of Rabat, half-covered with huge ramshackle clematis and dark red roses, old Ingoldby read Miss White's letter.

Then, holding it, he walked into his garden and stood by the well and read it again, looking up at last to regard the great clumps of lilies all about his feet. 'Gone crackers,' he said.

Then he went in and poured himself a bowl of cornflakes and took it into the garden to eat. It was one of the things the Maltese knew about him and rather respected. The old Maltese, that is, the ones who remembered the eccentric pink-faced English roaring about. They often ate cornflakes in the garden, played bagpipes on their roof-tops, blustered over whisky and became obsessive about the difficulty of growing sweet peas, while their thin, sweet-natured wives talked over tea-trolleys. Malta had been gentle to the English wives. For some mysterious reason the Maltese women and the English women had loved and understood each other, respected each other's religion, liked each other's children. Mistresses and maids had wept at parting when terms of Service were up and the ships had gone sailing home.

But old Ingoldby had never had a wife. He'd been RN until the end and been about a bit of course, but he'd kept away from women. Kept away from most people after retirement. Lived in the lop-sided ancient house and painted. He knew Malta better than any Maltese. He knew a stream on it, a small river, though all the guide books said there was none. He painted on the south shore, taking his gear in the back of a battered old Ford, walking laden with it over little plots of vineyard above the threads sewn over the earth to keep the birds away, leaping on now rather stiff old legs a chasm between rocks with purple sea beneath them, totally alone, watched only by one or two men lying on their stomachs with guns, hunting larks, he painted endlessly the sea. Miss White's fortnight's visit, just over, had disrupted his life very little. She had stayed at a good, quiet hotel in St George's Bay, meeting him for supper now and then. Twice he had taken her for a drive. He was not actively missing her.

'Crackers,' he said again at lunch time on the rock, taking out a packet of old-fashioned egg sandwiches wrapped tightly in greaseproof paper with envelope ends. 'Off her rocker. It's not allowed.'

He was scarcely younger than Miss White. He had been one of her first and older pupils. He had never forgotten her and had written to her all his life, at sea, during the First and Second Wars, from his shore-station, from Malta in his retirement – always for Christmas and Easter. She sent him tea-cloths on his birthday and handkerchieves and a copy of the school magazine. He had never found her female or attractive or even wise but nevertheless, though he did not know it, he loved her and she was the only woman he had ever felt his own.

'What's the ruling on sending flowers to England these days?' he asked in the shop in the village – to very great amazement.

'*Exporting?*' they said.

'No. Sending a present.'

'You're allowed to take a bunch,' they said. 'People do sometimes. Just like you can still sometimes bring in pheasants.'

'There was English families over St Julian's who used to take in potatoes.' Everyone laughed and smiled.

'Wouldn't happen now,' said an old Maltese lady in Maltese, swelling in a dark corner like bread. She blinked straight ahead of her, looking at old tourists and their babies, now parents themselves who never came back, remembering all the blonde hair and the buckets and spades and how the English children had loved the Maltese sticky sweets. The streets had been packed then not only with holiday people but with the proper English Maltese who loved Malta.

'I want to send a parcel of Easter lilies to England,' said the Captain. 'I thought I would send them with someone going over. Someone might consent to carry a bundle just over the arm. Not many – say fifty. Packed tight they would be no trouble.'

The shop was bewildered, but being Maltese did not show it. They smiled dazzlingly and agreed that it was a beautiful idea. Somebody said that the Captain ought to find out about a permit. He ought to go in to Valletta, they said, glittering happily at him, knowing that he had not been to Sliema for years, let alone Valletta.

The Captain said yes, and went away so helplessly that an old man sitting on a kitchen chair outside the shop playing patience, looked up and said that if the Captain liked, his son could drive to Valletta tomorrow and a woman – the granddaughter of the shop, huge with a great-grandchild to come, ran after him and said, 'No – you leave it to us, Captain. Leave it to us. We have a nephew in the Customs and Excise. Buy the lilies and tell us when.'

*

Dear Miss White.

Thank you for your letter. I am more than glad that you enjoyed your holiday here and found Malta still pleasant after so many changes and so long. We must not let so many years pass before you visit us again. For my part, seeing you again, you who taught me manners, was as always a very great pleasure.

As to the query about lilies, although at first very doubtful that there would be any chance of export, owing to the cool relationships between governments and the endless formalities in such matters, I hear from Maltese friends that one bunch of flowers, taken as a gift, is in order. A difficulty might obtain at your end as plants are prohibited imports to Britain. If however we make sure that there are no *bulbs* attached to the lilies and I can get the necessary note from the Powers that Be, I think I might be able to arrange something.

Certainly fifty pence per bloom sounds very ridiculous even for England and one would like to do something to help.

Will you write and instruct me exactly when the lilies will be needed? I imagine that you will want them on Easter Saturday. I shall probably be able to send them via my old friend Sir Henry Hatt – they travel home annually on Easter Saturday as he likes to attend his old church on Easter Day and afterwards spends the summer at home. His wife I have to admit may *not* be co-operative but I shall do my best with Henry. I should like precise details of the arrangements for collection at London airport and will send details of the estimated time of arrival of the Hatts' flight. Fortunately there is still time for us to make all our plans water-tight.

The weather here is continuing to be beautiful and I have been painting unhindered all week. Your visit in no way hampered the picture's progress and this is being a most successful spring. Your stay, as ever, brought only pleasure. Sincerely yours Paul Ingoldby.

*

My dear Paul,

How very good of you to take my request for Easter lilies so seriously. Alas, here at All Saints they are very uncertain of the sense of it and proceeding with the purchase of expensive lilies as before. I feel more and more that there is a great lack of imagination, spirit and *go* about this country nowadays and I have therefore stuck to my guns in the hope of a change of policy in future years. I am enclosing a cheque for £1 (one pound) and intend to meet the lilies myself on Easter Saturday and bring them directly back from the airport to arrange them in the church. I shall have completed my church work for Easter Day before I set out.

This will not be a particularly joyful Easter at All Saints incidentally, as the new Team Vicar has told us – just this week – the sad news that the church is to be closed down. The main reason is that the roof needs several thousand pounds spending on it. There are several other churches in the town and poor Father Banks is worked off his feet. Or so they say. He seems to me to be very seldom on them on account of all his committee meetings. I often wonder how these parsons would get on if they had had to stand before a class of children for six hours a day – *and* take games and supervise dinners. Better perhaps. But as to All Saints, we are all fairly poor now and we have given all we can over the past years – our jewellery, silver bits and pieces and between ourselves I have even given away the needlework picture of my great-grandfather the admiral. I know that I have bored you with all this for far too long when I was with you, and you are not, dear Paul, and never were even as a child, in any way religious. I remember to this day your stony stare when we were doing the Sermon on the Mount. But you will understand because you have a kind heart that the closure of All Saints where I was baptised as were my parents and grandparents (my grandfather of course was the first churchwarden) and where so many of us, and *not* only the old, spend a very great deal of time and prayer, will be a blow. It is not a beautiful building but it stands in blocks of identical suburban streets, all so dull, all so tasteful, all with the same expensive curtain linings to the windows and the same flicker of the television screen, all silent of life otherwise as one walks the dog late at night, that it stands out as something different and serious and I truly believe that temples of worship are needed by man as I said when we spent the delightful day driving to the golden temples of Hagar Qum.

Well, dear Paul, I am nearly eighty years old so that I shan't be in need of the building or any building much longer in any case, but I am very glad to be able to make some gesture of – well, of positive farewell in the matter of the lilies, and I am grateful to you for that. As to your kind remarks about it being I who taught you manners that is rubbish. It was your Nannie taught you manners – a very nice woman. I remember her. A very good sort. Many

Methodists of course can be good Christians. Your sincere friend Clara White.

*

'Lilies?' said Lady Hatt.

'Just a bunch of lilies.'

'What – to carry? *Hand* baggage?'

'Yes. Nothing at all really,' said Sir Henry nervously. His skin was like old porridge and he was hunched up in an ancient arm chair at the Xara Palace Hotel where he had lived for twenty years in a daze of memory and for five years trying not to see his new wife who slept in another room. She had been his nurse, and their marriage those few years ago had seemed a good arrangement. Vermilion trouser-suited, with spectacularly waved hair and a face painted into a 1940s mask, she was flinging pearls round her neck and prodding earrings in to her ears. She twisted her face about in mimic agony and stared with fierce eyes at him through the mirror.

'Who will carry them? Whatever is it all about?'

'Well, you will hardly have to carry them at all. Nobody will. Someone will hand them to you at the airport and the steward will put them on the rack for you. At London the steward will get them down again and you will simply have to carry them through customs and hand them to this old friend of Ingoldby. There's a permit – all has been seen to. They're for a church at Easter.'

'And all is left to me?'

'I intended to take them. I can't help being unable to come. It is the doctor –'

'I don't dispute you can't come. Just as you don't dispute I have to go –'

'No, no.'

'I have to open up the house. For when you are well. I am ready to do this for you and to come back and fetch you. But I don't see why I should take these – bloody – lilies.'

He drooped in the faded velvet chair and the Maltese light shone through the window and the leaves of a vine. His paper-pale face sagged. Her brilliant trouser-suit and white frothy blouse glared in the old room, with its old stone walls. 'The car has come,' he said.

She kissed the top of his shiny, freckly head in a businesslike way and straightened his rug. 'Old Ingoldby'll come and see you. You'll be all right.' She fiddled at the catch of her pearls round the front of her neck, ands then with a big diamond brooch. He said, suddenly urgent, shaky, 'Take the lilies.'

*

Miss White at about the same moment was settling her dog with a bowl of water and checking windows and doors. She then put on her gloves and hat and walked down the hill to the station. She changed to the underground at Earls Court – a long wait – and at last got in to a train direct to London Airport. It was an excellent train, new and bright and clean, and she was in no way over-excited by it for it had served her very well earlier in the year on the way to her holiday.

She felt odder, though, than then. Rather weak. Her feet prickled. They did not quite touch the floor. Her heart beat very loud and to try both to still it and to distract attention from her distress – as she had done since she was a child – she grinned her zany grin about the carriage. The few people lolling opposite, this Easter Saturday afternoon, took little notice.

She reached the airport far too soon and thought that she would find a cup of tea, and it was while she was standing with her tray for the tea that the pain hit her in the chest like the piercing of a sharp knife. She bent over the tray and had to stand still. There was a wide space between her and the cash desk, but she could not go on. People behind her – it was quiet at the airport today – the rush had been yesterday (Good Friday – to travel on Good Friday!) – people behind her took their trays round her back, not looking at her. I could die here, she thought, and no one would notice. She thought of a newspaper report of how somebody had died on London Airport and no one had noticed for seven hours.

Though why should it matter where one died? she thought. To Christians at any rate – taught at All Saints. 'Dying is only moving in to another room,' she said to the triangles of chocolate cake behind the glass boxes on the shelves.

After a while she slid the tray along to the cash desk and paid for the tea. Then, tottery, she made for a near table. The tray seemed heavy. She felt very small. I am very small, she thought. I have always been small. I have always thought of myself with – she paused, facing secret sin – well, with some sort of tall man near me.

She sat on the plastic orange bucket seat and her feet again did not quite touch the ground. She thought of Paul Ingoldby. Such a nice boy. She hung on to the safe thought that he was one of her boys. Her pupils. He must be ten years younger. She had been a new teacher of twenty and he had been a little boy of ten. They were now eighty and seventy. She thought of her letter to him. How that in some way it had not been proper. She had shown too much of her heart in it, she thought.

Then she thought, Oh dear Lord God if I had only sometimes shown more of my heart. She closed her eyes.

When at last the little letters made of green lights on the board above her head swam into place and said that the Malta flight had at last landed, she noticed how late it was. She had been sitting at the table for over an hour. She must have slept. At some point she must also have drunk the tea for her cup was empty.

'Landed' said the green lights, so she got up and went down the huge hall and, holding the rail, she climbed the stairs and walked back along the long stretch to the railing where people waited for the passengers.

There were not really many people but it was not easy for her to get up against the rope rail, so she walked back to the place where the airport attendants were keeping a space clear for the people coming off the plane to pass.

'Now then, Gran,' said one. 'Keep back now. You don't

want to be trampled under. You'll get lost.'

'I have to stand at the front,' said Miss White. 'You see, I'll know her but she won't know me.'

'How you going to know her?'

'She'll be carrying lilies.'

'Lilies. I doubt that,' said the man. 'Not allowed – lilies.'

'There is a permit,' said Miss White. 'It has all been properly cleared. It was arranged by a Captain in the Navy.'

'Navy, eh?' said the man watching Miss White's queer grin. 'Ah – boyfriend.'

Miss White's eighty-year-old lips set firm. Shocked, she turned away and saw Lady Hatt coming towards her, lurching a little, brick-red in the cheeks and vermilion in the body and on her face an expression of fierce malice. She was carrying her big bottle of duty-free whisky, a large crocodile handbag and her frothy blouse was escaping from the waist of her trouser suit, her hair untidy. Her over-thin legs above wobbly ankles tottered pathetically above high heels. In her arms as well as the whisky was a clutter of parcels, and between them and below the dangle of unsteady-looking earrings was a huge sheaf of newspaper from which stuck the heads of many tight-foiled, greyish lilies.

'*Oh*, how kind, how kind!' Miss White leapt forward. 'Oh how very kind of you!'

Lady Hatt glared. She shuffled the lilies off her heap of belongings and let them fall very heavily into Miss White's arms. An earring swung. She marched on.

Miss White ran after. 'Oh, please. I do want to thank you. I've brought some chocolates –'

'Oh – certainly not. *No* thank you.'

'I don't even know your name, so can't write –'

'I hardly think that's necessary at all.' Lady Hatt smelled of gin. Her eyes were cold hard blue, the whites reddish. She had released the lilies like a package of poison, and not quite knowing the source of her hate she seethed against them as she might have seethed at the touch of an angel's wing. She had been manipulated into the lilies – uncharacteristic emblems of other people's worlds. She had been manipulated into them by her husband whom she despised and for a cause she despised. 'Easter,' she thought. 'Churches. Women like this. Chocolates – my God!' She strode away – a chauffeur appearing from somewhere and taking her belongings and her overnight bag and her whisky. She disappeared leaving Miss White with the chocolates and the bundle.

'I so hope they weren't a trouble,' she said aloud – and at once realised that they must have been, for the bundle was large and bony and really extremely heavy. She cradled it in her arms and found that she could scarcely see over it. Going down the stairs, buffeted about – the airport was getting more crowded now – she found she could only go a step at a time as she could not spare a hand for the hand rail. Waiting at last on the platform for the underground train again, she tried to peer in to the top of the sheaf round the tight-packed pages of *The Times of Malta*, secured with firm string and excellent naval knotting. She thought, 'They don't look so beautiful after all. I hope –' and then the knife twisted in her chest again and she stood very still and closed her eyes and grinned very wide. When it had passed she said, 'I hope they'll improve when they're put in water.'

She took a taxi when she got to her own station. It was a dreadful extravagance but she felt unequal to the hill and it was now dark. A sweet, spring darkness and the cherry blossom smelling in all the suburban gardens. The blossom whitened in the April evening. In some rooms in the decorous streets lights were coming on. In some – really rather prettily, she thought, I don't know why I ever despised them – the lights of television sets flickered blue. Dark as it was someone was giving his patch of grass the first mowing of the year in St Agnes Road and the wet, summery, heart-breaking smell of the sap hit her as she stepped from the cab at the door of the church. It seemed the smell of all her life – the essence of the best of all her life – a new moon, she thought, suburban grass and summer coming. She thought how happy she had been in this place.

She had – as Sacristan of course she had – a key to the church and went in and felt for the light switches. She switched on the chancel light and the lady chapel and the light of the vestry. Looking at all the great arrangements of flowers shining to themselves through the night waiting for Easter morning, she grinned her grin and switched on every light in the place. There seemed, she thought, to be a great many lilies – two great vases on the altar and two more on the chancel steps. Pounds and pounds worth. Well of course they'd all gone silly. Bravado, she thought, sentimental bravado because the church was going to be closed.

They could have saved fifty pounds, she thought, towards the roof.

She put down the heavy pig lilies on the steps of the lady chapel and went looking for a vase or two behind the organ. There wasn't much left. Only the old green bucket thing that was always left till last and was usually stuck up at the back of the bookstall where it didn't show. She rummaged and found a great old glass jar – something to do with the Guides. She swilled both these out with water and took them back to the lady chapel.

Feeling now very tired, she undid – not easily – the traceries round *The Times of Malta* and let the lilies fall out loose, scatter and breathe on their hard dark stalks. She shook them and spread them until they lay released across the blue chapel carpet. Lying in their midst was a magnificent string of pearls.

'Her pearls!' thought Miss White. 'They must be Paul's friend's pearls. They must have dropped off. Oh, how very dreadful!'

She touched them with her finger tip. 'They are beautiful,' she thought. 'How dreadful. I must put them in the safe. She won't know what's happened to them.'

The pearls glowed among the lilies. The light of the vestry where the safe was, looked far away. Miss White looked at the lilies and then at the pearls and thought, 'The pearls are more beautiful. It ought not to be so. The lilies are weeds after all. And they are dead. I am old and a fool.'

Tears came into her eyes. For safety, she picked up the pearls and fastened them round her neck. 'I'd like to see them on,' she thought, 'I love pearls.' But the glass where Father Banks looked at himself and his vestments over in the vestry before service, swinging about, handsome and grand (How different from Paul. If I had had Father Banks to teach he would not —), the glass was far away in the vestry, too.

'Vanity,' said Miss White to herself, and twisted the pearls out of sight under the collar of her old jersey. Then, feeling tireder still, she put down her round head among the pig lilies, and died.

*

She had left everything to the church, of course, and there was practically nothing except her small flat – and the pearls, which everyone was astonished to hear about. They were spectacular, said a sympathetic local jeweller, and he gave two thousand pounds for them. Lady Hatt, by the time Miss White's body had been found lying peaceful among the dead lilies on Easter morning, had had her hysterics, mounted her first wave of accusation against the airline and was well on the way with her claim to the insurance company, which was sticky but at length paid up. Paul Ingoldby did not hear for some time of his old teacher's death on Easter eve for she had left him no bequest, thinking it inappropriate. He felt satisfaction, however, when he heard that the lilies had reached their destination.

The church with its new roof survived.

The Pangs of Love

It is not generally known that the good little mermaid of Hans Christian Andersen, who died for love of the handsome prince and allowed herself to dissolve in the foam of the ocean, had a younger sister, a difficult child of very different temper.

She was very young when the tragedy occurred, and was only told it later by her five elder sisters and her grandmother, the Sea King's mother with the twelve important oyster shells in her tail. They spent much of their time, all these women, mourning the tragic life of the little mermaid in the Sea King's palace below the waves, and a very dreary place it had become in consequence.

'I don't see what she did it for,' the seventh little mermaid used to say. 'Love for a man – ridiculous,' and all the others would sway on the tide and moan, 'Hush, hush – you don't know how she suffered for love.'

'I don't understand this "suffered for love," ' said the seventh mermaid. 'She sounds very silly and obviously spoiled her life.'

'She may have spoiled her life,' said the Sea King's mother, 'but think how good she was. She was given the chance of saving her life, but because it would have harmed the prince and his earthly bride she let herself die.'

'What had he done so special to deserve that?' asked the seventh mermaid.

'He had *done* nothing. He was just her beloved prince to whom she would sacrifice all.'

'What did he sacrifice for her?' asked Signorina Settima.

'Not a lot,' said the Sea King's mother, 'I believe they

'don't on the whole. But it doesn't stop us loving them.'

'It would me,' said the seventh mermaid. 'I must get a look at some of this mankind, and perhaps I will then understand more.'

'You must wait until your fifteenth birthday,' said the Sea King's mother. 'That has always been the rule with all your sisters.'

'Oh, shit,' said the seventh mermaid (she was rather coarse). 'Times change. I'm as mature now as they were at fifteen. Howsabout tomorrow?'

'I'm sure I don't know what's to be done with you,' said the Sea King's mother, whose character had weakened in later years. 'You are totally different from the others and yet I'm sure I brought you all up the same.'

'Oh no you didn't,' said the five elder sisters in chorus, 'she's always been spoiled. We'd never have dared talk to you like that. Think if our beloved sister who died for love had talked to you like that.'

'Maybe she should have done,' said the dreadful seventh damsel officiously, and this time in spite of her grand-mother's failing powers she was put in a cave for a while in the dark and made to miss her supper.

Nevertheless, she was the sort of girl who didn't let other people's views interfere with her too much, and she could argue like nobody else in the sea, so that in the end her grandmother said, 'Oh for goodness' sake then – go. Go now and don't even wait for your *fourteenth* birthday. Go and look at some men and don't come back unless they can turn you into a mermaid one hundredth part as good as your beloved foamy sister.'

'Whoops,' said Mademoiselle Sept, and she flicked her tail and was away up out of the Sea King's palace, rising through the coral and the fishes that wove about the red and blue seaweed trees like birds, up and up until her head shot out into the air and she took a deep breath of it and said, 'Wow!'

The sky, as her admirable sister had noticed stood above the sea like a large glass bell, and the waves rolled and lifted and tossed towards a green shore where there were fields and palaces and flowers and forests where fish with wings and legs wove about the branches of green and so forth trees, singing at the tops of their voices. On a balcony sticking out from the best palace stood, as he had stood before his marriage when the immaculate sister had first seen him, the wonderful prince with his chin resting on his hand as it often did of an evening – and indeed in the mornings and afternoons, too.

'Oh help!' said the seventh mermaid, feeling a queer twisting around the heart. Then she thought, 'Watch it.' She dived under water for a time and came up on a rock on the shore, where she sat and examined her sea-green finger nails and smoothed down the silver scales of her tail.

She was sitting where the prince could see her and after a while he gave a cry and she looked up. 'Oh,' he said, 'how you remind me of someone. I thought for a moment you were my lost love.'

'Lost love,' said the seventh mermaid. 'And whose fault was that? She was my sister. She died for love of you and you never gave her one serious thought. You even took her along on your honeymoon like a pet toy. I don't know what she saw in you.'

'I always loved her,' said the prince. 'But I didn't realise it until too late.'

'That's what they all say,' said Numera Septima. 'Are you a poet? They're the worst. Hardy, Tennyson, Shakespeare, Homer. Homer was the worst of all. And he hadn't a good word to say for mermaids.'

'Forgive me,' said the prince, who had removed his chin from his hand and was passionately clenching the parapet. 'Every word you speak reminds me more and more –'

'I don't see how it can,' said the s.m., 'since for love of you and because she was told it was the only way she could come to you, she let them cut out her tongue, the silly ass.'

'And your face,' he cried, 'your whole aspect, except of course for the tail.'

'She had that removed, too. They told her it would be agony and it was, so my sisters tell me. It shrivelled up and she got two ugly stumps called legs – I dare say you've got

37

them under that parapet. When she danced, every step she took was like knives.'

'Alas, alas!'

'Catch me getting rid of my tail,' said syedmaya krasavitsa, twitching it seductively about, and the prince gave a great spring from the balcony and embraced her on the rocks. It was all right until half way down but the scales were cold and prickly. Slimy, too, and he shuddered.

'How dare you shudder,' cried La Septième. 'Go back to your earthly bride.'

'She's not here at present,' said the p., 'she's gone to her mother for the weekend. Won't you come in? We can have dinner in the bath.'

The seventh little mermaid spent the whole weekend with the prince in the bath, and he became quite frantic with desire by Monday morning because of the insurmountable problem below the mermaid's waist. 'Your eyes, your hair,' he cried, 'but that's about all.'

'My sister did away with her beautiful tail for love of you,' said the s.m., reading a volume of Descartes over the prince's shoulder as he lay on her sea-green bosom. 'They tell me she even wore a disgusting harness on the top half of her for you, and make-up and dresses. She was the saint of mermaids.'

'Ah, a saint,' said the prince. 'But without your wit, your spark. I would do anything in the world for you.'

'So what about getting rid of your legs?'

'Getting rid of my *legs*?'

'Then you can come and live with me below the waves. No one has legs down there and there's nothing wrong with any of us. As a matter of fact, aesthetically we're a very good species.'

'Get rid of my *legs*?'

'Yes – my grandmother, the Sea King's mother, and the Sea Witch behind the last whirlpool who fixed up my poor sister, silly cow, could see to it for you.'

'Oh, how I love your racy talk,' said the prince. 'It's like nothing I ever heard before. I should love you even with my eyes shut. Even at a distance. Even on the telephone.'

'No fear,' said the seventh m., 'I know all about this waiting by the telephone. All my sisters do it. It never rings when they want it to. It has days and days of terrible silence and they all roll about weeping and chewing their handkerchieves. You don't catch me getting in that condition.'

'Gosh, you're marvellous,' said the prince, who had been to an old-fashioned school, 'I'll do anything –'

'The legs?'

'Hum. Ha. Well – the legs.'

'Carry me back to the rocks,' said the seventh little mermaid, 'I'll leave you to think about it. What's more I hear a disturbance in the hall which heralds the return of your wife. By the way, it wasn't your wife, you know, who saved you from drowning when you got ship-wrecked on your sixteenth birthday. It was my dear old sister once again. "She swam among the spars and planks which drifted on the sea, quite forgetting they might crush her. Then she ducked beneath the water, and rising again on the billows managed at last to reach you who by now" (being fairly feeble in the muscles I'd guess, with all the stately living) "was scarcely able to swim any longer in the raging sea. Your arms, your legs" (ha!) "began to fail you and your beautiful eyes were closed and you must surely have died if my sister had not come to your assistance. She held your head above the water and let the billows drive her and you together wherever they pleased." '

'What antique phraseology.'

'It's a translation from the Danish. Anyway, "when the sun rose red and beaming from the water, your cheeks regained the hue of life but your eyes remained closed. My sister kissed –"

('No!')

' "– your lofty handsome brow and stroked back your wet locks. . . . She kissed you again and longed that you might live." What's more if you'd only woken up then she could have spoken to you. It was when she got obsessed by you back down under the waves again that she went in for all this tongue and tail stuff with the Sea Witch.'

'She was an awfully nice girl,' said the prince, and tears

came into his eyes – which was more than they ever could do for a mermaid however sad, because as we know from H. C. Andersen, mermaids can never cry which makes it harder for them.

'The woman I saw when I came to on the beach,' said the prince, 'was she who is now my wife. A good sort of woman but she drinks.'

'I'm not surprised,' said the seventh mermaid. 'I'd drink if I was married to someone who just stood gazing out to sea thinking of a girl he had allowed to turn into foam,' and she flicked her tail and disappeared.

'Now then,' she thought, 'what's to do next?' She was not to go back, her grandmother had said, until she was one hundredth part as good as the little m. her dead sister, now a spirit of air, and although she was a tearaway and, as I say, rather coarse, she was not altogether untouched by the discipline of the Sea King's mother and her upbringing. Yet she could not say that she exactly yearned for her father's palace with all her melancholy sisters singing dreary stuff about the past. Nor was she too thrilled to return to the heaviness of water with all the featherless fishes swimming through the amber windows and butting in to her, and the living flowers growing out of the palace walls like dry rot. However, after flicking about for a bit, once coming up to do an inspection of a fishing boat in difficulties with the tide and enjoying the usual drop-jawed faces, she took a header home into the front room and sat down quietly in a corner.

'You're back,' said the Sea King's mother. 'How was it? I take it you now feel you are a hundredth part as good as your sainted sister?'

'I've always tried to be good,' said the s.m., 'I've just tried to be rationally good and not romantically good, that's all.'

'Now don't start again. I take it you have seen some men?'

'I saw the prince.'

At this the five elder sisters set up a wavering lament.

'Did you feel for him –'

'Oh, feelings, feelings,' said the seventh and rational mermaid, 'I'm sick to death of feelings. He's good looking, I'll give you that, and rather sweet-natured and he's having a rough time at home, but he's totally self-centred. I agree that my sister must have been a true sea-saint to listen to him dripping on about himself all day. He's warm-hearted though, and not at all bad in the bath.'

The Sea King's mother fainted away at this outspoken and uninhibited statement, and the five senior mermaids fled in shock. The seventh mermaid tidied her hair and set off to find the terrible cave of the Sea Witch behind the last whirlpool, briskly pushing aside the disgusting polypi, half plant, half animal, and the fingery seaweeds that had so terrified her dead sister on a similar journey.

'Aha,' said the Sea Witch, stirring a pot of filthy black bouillabaisse, 'you, like your sister, cannot do without me. I suppose you also want to risk body and soul for the human prince up there on the dry earth?'

'Good afternoon, no,' said the seventh mermaid. 'Might I sit down?' (For even the seventh mermaid was polite to the Sea Witch.) 'I want to ask you if, when the prince follows me down here below the waves, you could arrange for him to live with me until the end of time?'

'He'd have to lose his legs. What would he think of that?'

'I think he might consider it. In due course.'

'He would have to learn to sing and not care about clothes or money or possessions or power – what would he think of that?'

'Difficult, but not impossible.'

'He'd have to face the fact that if you fell in love with one of your own kind and married him he would die and also lose his soul as your sister did when he wouldn't make an honest woman of her.'

'It was not,' said the seventh mermaid, 'that he wouldn't make an honest woman of her. It just never occurred to him. After all – she couldn't speak to him about it. You had cut out her tongue.'

'Aha,' said the s.w., 'it's different for a man, is it? Falling in love, are you?

'Certainly not,' said Fräulein Sieben. 'Certainly not.'

'Cruel then, eh? Revengeful? Or do you hate men? It's very fashionable.'

'I'm not cruel. Or revengeful. I'm just rational. And I don't hate men. I think I'd probably like them very much, especially if they are all as kind and as beautiful as the prince. I just don't believe in falling in love with them. It is a burden and it spoils life. It is a mental illness. It killed my sister and it puts women in a weak position and makes us to be considered second class.'

'They fall in love with us,' said the Sea Witch. 'That's to say, with women. So I've been told. Sometimes. Haven't you read the sonnets of Shakespeare and the poems of Petrarch?'

'The sonnets of Shakespeare are hardly all about one woman,' said the bright young mermaid. 'In fact some of them are written to a man. As for Petrarch, (there was scarcely a thing this girl hadn't read) he only saw his girl once, walking over a bridge. They never exactly brushed their teeth together.'

'Well, there are the Brownings.'

'Yes. The Brownings were all right,' said the mermaid. 'Very funny looking though. I don't suppose anyone else ever wanted them.'

'You are a determined young mermaid,' said the Sea Witch. 'Yes, I'll agree to treat the prince if he comes this way. But you must wait and see if he does.'

'Thank you, yes I will,' said the seventh mermaid. 'He'll come,' and she did wait, quite confidently, being the kind of girl well-heeled men do run after because she never ran after them, very like Elizabeth Bennet.

So, one day, who should come swimming down through the wonderful blue water and into the golden palaces of the Sea King and floating through the windows like the fish and touching with wonder the dry-rot flowers upon the walls, but the prince, his golden hair floating behind him and his golden hose and tunic stuck tight to him all over like a wet-suit, and he looked terrific.

'Oh, princess, sweet seventh mermaid,' he said, finding her at once (because she was the sort of girl who is always in the right place at the right time). 'I have found you again. Ever since I threw you back in the sea I have dreamed of you.

I cannot live without you. I have left my boozy wife and have come to live with you for ever.'

'There are terrible conditions,' said the seventh mermaid. 'Remember. The same conditions which my poor sister accepted in reverse. You must lose your legs and wear a tail.'

'This I will do.'

'You must learn to sing for hours and hours in unison with the other mermen, in wondrous notes that hypnotise simple sailors up above and make them think they hear faint sounds from Glyndebourne or Milan.'

'As to that,' said the prince, 'I always wished I had a voice.'

'And you must know that if I decide that I want someone more than you, someone of my own sort, and marry him, you will lose everything, as my sister did – your body, your immortal soul and your self-respect.'

'Oh well, that's quite all right,' said the prince. He knew that no girl could ever prefer anyone else to him.

'*Right*,' said the mermaid. 'Well, before we go off to the Sea Witch, let's give a party. And let me introduce you to my mother and sisters.'

Then there followed a time of most glorious celebration, similar only to the celebration some years back for the prince's wedding night when the poor little mermaid now dead had had to sit on the deck of the nuptial barque and watch the bride and groom until she had quite melted away. Then the cannons had roared and the flags had waved and a royal bridal tent of cloth of gold and purple and precious furs had been set upon the deck and when it grew dark, coloured lamps had been lit and sailors danced merrily and the bride and groom had gone into the tent without the prince giving the little mermaid a backward glance.

Now, beneath the waves the sea was similarly alight with glowing corals and brilliant sea-flowers and a bower was set up for the seventh mermaid and the prince and she danced with all the mermen who had silver crowns on their heads and St Christophers round their necks, very trendy like the South of France, and they all had a lovely time.

And the party went on and on. It was beautiful. Day after

day and night after night and anyone who was anyone was there, and the weather was gorgeous – no storms below or above and it was exactly as Hans Christian Andersen said: 'a wondrous blue tint lay over everything; one would be more inclined to fancy one was high up in the air and saw nothing but sky above and below than that one was at the bottom of the sea. During a calm, too, one could catch a glimpse of the sun. It looked like a crimson flower from the cup of which, light streamed forth.' The seventh mermaid danced and danced, particularly with a handsome young merman with whom she seemed much at her ease.

'Who is that merman?' asked the prince. 'You seem to know him well.'

'Oh – just an old friend,' said the seventh m., 'he's always been about. We were in our prams together.' (This was not true. The seventh m. was just testing the prince. She had never bothered with mermen even in her pram.)

'I'm sorry said the prince, 'I can't have you having mermen friends. Even if there's nothing in it.'

'We must discuss this with the Sea Witch,' said the seventh mermaid, and taking his hand she swam with him out of the palace and away and away through the dreadful polypi again. She took him past the last whirlpool to the cave where the Sea Witch was sitting eating a most un-pleasant-looking type of caviar from a giant snail shell and stroking her necklace of sea snakes.

'Ha,' said the Sea Witch, 'the prince. You have come to be rid of your legs?'

'Er – well –'

'You have come to be rid of your earthly speech, your clothes and possessions and power?'

'Well, it's something that we might discuss.'

'And you agree to lose soul and body and self-respect if this interesting mermaid goes off and marries someone?'

There was a very long silence and the seventh mermaid closely examined some shells round her neck, tiny pale pink oyster shells each containing a pearl which would be the glory of a Queen's crown. The prince held his beautiful chin in his lovely, sensitive hand. His gentle eyes filled with tears.

At last he took the mermaid's small hand and kissed its palm and folded the sea-green nails over the kiss (he had sweet ways) and said, 'I must not look at you. I must go at once,' and he pushed off. That is to say, he pushed himself upwards off the floor of the sea and shot up and away and away through the foam, arriving home in time for tea and early sherry with his wife, who was much relieved.

*

It was a very long time indeed before the seventh little mermaid returned to the party. In fact the party was all but over. There was only the odd slithery merman twanging a harp of dead fisherman's bones and the greediest and grubbiest of the deep water fishes eating up the last of the sandwiches. The Sea King's old mother was asleep, her heavy tail studded with important oyster shells coiled round the legs of her throne.

The five elder sisters had gone on somewhere amusing.

The seventh mermaid sat down at the feet of her grandmother and at length the old lady woke up and surveyed the chaos left over from the fun. 'Hullo, my child,' she said. 'Are you alone?'

'Yes. The prince has gone. The engagement's off.'

'My dear – what did I tell you? Remember how your poor sister suffered. I warned you.'

'Pooh – I'm not suffering. I've just proved my point. Men aren't worth it.'

'Maybe you and she were unfortunate,' said the Sea King's mother. 'Which men you meet is very much a matter of luck, I'm told.'

'No – they're all the same,' said the mermaid who by now was nearly fifteen years old. 'I've proved what I suspected. I'm free now – free of the terrible pangs of love which put women in bondage, and I shall dedicate my life to freeing and instructing other women and saving them from humiliation.'

'Well, I hope you don't become one of those frowsty little women who don't laugh and have only one subject of conversation,' said the Sea Witch. 'It is a mistake to base a whole philosophy upon one disappointment.'

'Disappointment – pah!' said the seventh mermaid. 'When was I ever negative?'

'And I hope you don't become aggressive.'

'When was I ever aggressive?' said Senorita Septima ferociously.

'That's a good girl then,' said the Sea King's mother, 'So now – unclench that fist.'

Stone Trees

So now that he is dead so now that he is dead I am to spend the day with them. The Robertsons.

On the Isle of Wight. Train journey train journey from London. There and back in a day.

So now that he is dead –

They were at the funeral. Not their children. Too little. So good so good they were to me. She – Anna – she cried a lot. Tom held my arm tight. Strong. I liked it. In the place even the place where your coffin was, I liked it, his strong arm. Never having liked Tom that much, I liked his strong arm.

And they stayed over. Slept at the house a night or two. Did the telephone. Some gran or someone was with their children. Thank God we had no children. Think of Tom/ Anna dying and those two children left –

So now that you are dead –

It's nice of them isn't it now that you are dead? Well, you'd have expected it. You aren't surprised by it. I'm not surprised by it. After all there has to be somewhere to go. All clean all clean at home. Back work soon someday. Very soon now for it's a week. They broke their two week holiday for the funeral. Holiday Isle of Wight where you/I went once. There was a dip, a big-dipper dip, a wavy line of cliffs along the shore, and in this dip of the cliffs a hotel – a long beach and the waves moving in shallow.

Over stone trees.

But it was long ago and what can stone trees have been? Fantasy.

So now that you are dead so now –

47

Sweetie love so now that you are dead I am to spend the day with the Robertsons alone and we shall talk you/I later. So now –

The boat crosses. Has crossed. Already. Criss-cross deck. Criss-cross water. Splashy sea and look –! Lovely clouds flying (now that you are dead) and here's the pier. A long, long pier into the sea and gulls shouting and children yelling here and there and here's my ticket and there they stand. All in a row – Tom, Anna, the two children solemn. And smiles now – Tom and Anna. Tom and Anna look too large to be quite true. Too good. Anna who never did anything wrong. Arms stretch too far forward for a simple day.

They stretch because they want. They would not stretch to me if you were obvious and not just dead. Then it would have been, hullo, easy crossing? Good. Wonderful day. Let's get back and down on the beach. Great to see you both.

So now that you are dead –

We paced last week. Three.

Tom. Anna. I.

And other black figures wood-faced outside the crematorium in blazing sun, examining shiny black-edged tickets on blazing bouquets. 'How good of Marjorie – fancy old Marjorie. I didn't even know she –' There was that woman who ran out of the so-called service with handkerchief at her eyes. But who was there except you my darling and I and the Robertsons and the shiny cards and did they do it then? Were they doing it then as we read the flowers? Do they do it at once or stack it up with other coffins and was it still inside waiting as I paced with portly Tom? Christian Tom – Tom we laughed at so often and oh my darling now that you are dead –

Cambridge. You can't say that Tom has precisely changed since Cambridge. Thickened. More solid. Unshaken still, quite unshaken and – well, wonderful of course. Anna hasn't changed. Small, specs, curly hair, straight-laced. Dear Anna how we sat and worked out all. Analysed. Girton. We talked about how many men it was decent to do it with without being wild and when you should decide to start and Anna said none and never. Not before marriage you said. Anna always in that church where Tom preached and Tom never looking Anna's way, and how she ached. So now that –

Sweet I miss you so. Now that you are –. My darling oh my God!

In the train two young women. (Yes thanks Anna, I'm fine. Nice journey. First time out. It's doing me good. Isn't it a lovely day?) There were these two women talking about their rights. They were reading about all that was due to them. In a magazine.

'Well, it's only right isn't it?'

'What?'

'Having your own life. Doing your thing.'

'Well –'

'Not – you know. Men and that. Not letting them have all the freedom and that. You have to stand up for yourself and get free of men.'

*

We come to the hotel and of course it is the one. The one in the dip of the cliffs almost on the beach, and how were they to know? It's typical though, somehow. We didn't like them my darling did we, after Cambridge very much? We didn't see them – dropped them in some way. We didn't see them for nearly two years. And we wondered, sometimes, whatever it was we had thought we had had in common – do-good, earnest Tom, healthy face and shorts, striding out over mountains singing snatches of Berlioz and stopping now and then to pray. And you were you and always unexpected – alert, alive, mocking and forever young and now that you are –

But they were there again. In California. You at the university and I at the university, teaching a term; and there – behold the Robertsons, holding out their arms to save America. Little house full of the shiny-faced, the chinless – marriage counsellors, marriage-enrichment classes oh my God! And one child in Anna and one just learning to walk.

49

We were taken to them by somebody just for a lark not knowing who they'd turn out to be and we said – 'Hey! Tom and Anna.'

And in Sacramento in a house with lacy balconies and little red Italian brick walls and all their old Cambridge books about and photographs we half-remembered, we opened wine and were very happy; and over the old white-washed fireplace there was Tom's old crucifix and his Cambridge oar. And I sat in the rocking chair she'd had at Girton and it felt familiar and we loved the Robertsons that day in sweaty, wheezing Sacramento because they were there again. This is no reason. But it is true.

We talked about how we'd all met each other first. Terrible party. Jesus College. Anna met Tom and I met you my darling and it was something or other – Feminism, Neo-Platonism, Third World – and there you were with bright, ridiculous, marvellous, mocking eyes and long hard hands and I loved you as everyone else clearly loved you. And the Robertsons talked sagely to one another. They were not the Robertsons then but Tom and Anna. We never became the anythings, thank God. There was no need because we were whatever the appearance might be one person and had no need of a plural term and now that –

Sweetie, do you remember the *smell* of that house? In Cambridge? And again in Sacramento? She liked it you know. She left dishes for a week and food bits and old knickers and tights in rolls on the mantelpiece and said, 'There are things more important.' Under the burning ethic there was you know something very desperate about Anna. Tom didn't notice her. Day after day and I'd guess night after night. He sat in the rocking chair and glared at God. And meeting them again just the same, in Sacramento, you looked at the crucifix and the oar and at me, your eyes like the first time we met because there we both remembered the first time, long ago. Remembering that was a short return to each other because by then, by America, I knew that you were one I'd never have to myself because wherever you were or went folk turned and smiled at you and loved you. Well, I'd known always. I didn't face it at first, that one woman would never be enough for you and that if I moved in with you you would soon move on.

Everyone wanted you. When we got married there was a general sense of comedy and the sense of my extraordinary and very temporary luck.

It is not right or dignified to love so much. To let a man rule so much. It is obsession and not love, a mental illness not a life. And of course, with marriage came the quarrelling and pain because I knew there were so many others, and you not coming home, and teasing when you did and saying that there was only me but of course I knew it was not so because of – cheap and trite things like – the smell of scent. It was worst just before the Robertsons went away.

But then – after California – we came here to this beach once and it was September like now, and a still, gold peace. And the hotel in the dip, and the sand white and wide and rock pools. And only I with you. You were quieter. You brought no work. You lay on the beach with a novel flapping pages and the sand gathering in them. We held hands and it was not as so often. It was not as when I looked at you and saw your eyes looking at someone else invisible. God, love – the killing sickness. Maybe never let it start – just mock and talk of Rights. Don't let it near. Sex without sentiment. Manage one's life with dignity. But now that you are dead –

And one day on that year's peaceful holiday we walked out to the stone trees which now I remember. They told us, at the hotel, that in the sea, lying on their stone sides, on their stone bark and broken stone branches, were great prehistoric trees, petrified and huge and broken into sections by the millenia and chopped here and there as by an infernal knife, like rhubarb chunks or blocks of Edinburgh candy, sand coloured, ancient among the young stones.

Trees so old that no one ever saw them living. Trees become stone. I said, 'I love stone,' and you said, 'I love trees,' and kicked them. You said, 'Who wants stone trees?' And we walked about on them, a stone stick forest, quite out to sea, and sat and put our feet in pools where green grasses swayed and starfish shone. And you said – despising the stone trees – there is only ever you-you know – and I knew that the last one was gone and the pain of her and you and I were one again. It was quite right that you loved so much being so much loved and I am glad, for now that you are dead –

I shall never see you any more.

I shall never feel your hand over my hand.

I shall never lean my head against you any more.

I shall never see your eyes which now that you are –

*

'The sandwiches are egg, love, and cheese, and there's chocolate. We didn't bring a feast. It's too hot.'

'It's lovely.'

'Drink?'

'I don't like Ribena, thanks.'

'It's not. It's wine. In tumblers. Today we're having a lot of wine in very big tumblers.'

(Anna Robertson of evangelical persuasion, who never acts extremely, is offering me wine in tumblers. Now that you are dead.)

'It's nice wine. I'll be drunk.'

The children say, 'You can have some of our cake. D'you want a biscuit?' They've been told to be nice. The little girl pats sand, absorbed, solemn, straight-haired, grave like Tom. The older one, the boy, eats cake and lies on his stomach aware of me and that my husband has died and gone to God.

And you have gone to God?

You were with God and you were my god and now that you –

The boy has long legs. Seven-year-old long legs. The boy is a little like you and not at all like Tom. He rolls over and gives me a biscuit. I'm so glad we had no children. I could not have shared you with children. We needed nobody else except you needed other girls to love a bit and leave – nothing important. You moved on and never mind. I didn't. I did not mind. The pain passed and I don't mind and I shall not mind now that you are dead.

The boy is really – or am I going mad altogether – very like you.

The boy is Peter.

Says, 'Are you coming out on the rocks?'

'I'm fine thanks, Peter. I'm drinking my wine.'

'Drink it later and come out on the rocks. Come on over the rocks.'

See Anna, Tom, proud of Peter being kind to me and only seven. They pretend not to see, fiddling with coffee flask, sun-tan oil. 'Wonderful summer,' says Anna.

'Wonderful.'

'Come on the rocks.'

'Peter – don't boss,' says Anna.

'Leave your wine and come,' says Peter, 'I'll show you the rocks.'

So I go with this boy over the rocks my darling now that you are dead and I have no child and I will never see you any more.

Not any more.

Ever again.

Now that you are –

It is ridiculous how this boy walks.

*

How Anna wept.

*

'Look, hold my hand,' says Peter, 'and take care. We're on old trees. What d'you think of that? They were so old they turned to stone. It's something in the atmosphere. They're awful, aren't they? I like trees all leafy and sparkly.'

'*Sparkly* trees?'

'Well, there'd be no pollution. No people. Now just rotten stone.'

'I like stone.'

He kicks them, 'I like trees.'

And I sit down my love because I will not see you any more or hold your hand or put my face on yours and this will pass of course. They've told me that this sort of grief will pass.

But I don't want the grief to change. I want not to forget the feel and look of you and the look of your live eyes and the physical life of you and I do not want to cease to grieve.

'Look, hey, look,' says Peter and stops balancing. 'The tide is coming in.' The water slaps. The dead stone which was once covered with breathing holes for life takes life again, and where it looked like burned out ashy stone there are colours, and little movements, and frondy things responding to water, which laps and laps.

'Look,' says Peter, 'there's a star-fish. Pink as pink. Hey – take my hand. Mind out. You mustn't slip.' (This boy has long hard hands.) 'The tide is coming in.'

*

How Anna cried.

*

The tide is coming in and it will cover the stone trees and then it will ebb back again and the stone trees will remain, and already the water is showing more growing things that are there all the time, though only now and then seen.

And Peter takes my hand in yours and I will never see you any more – How Anna cried. And things are growing in the cracks in the stones. The boy laughs and looks at me with your known eyes. Now that you are.

An Unknown Child

The bandaged della Robbia babies stretched their arms in blessing towards the piazza. Across the piazza the English-woman sat on a high window seat of the pensione and looked at them in the autumn evening light.

Her husband said, 'Come for dinner.'

'It's a wonderful evening. Look at the della Robbia babies. It's a pity about the traffic in between.'

'They'll want us to be in time for dinner. It's a pensione.'

'I'm glad the della Robbias are still there. They were there when I was twenty.'

'They were there when your grandmother was twenty. And her grandmother. And hers. We ought to go in for dinner.'

'Yes. Wait. I'm glad they haven't hacked them off the walls yet. They took the frescoes off the walls you know. Some sort of blotting paper. We'll see the marks where they used to be tomorrow. When I was here you could actually touch the frescoes. With your hands. Just going down the street. Like in the Renaissance. They survived the war but not the tourists. I'm glad they haven't hacked off the babies.'

*

Every bit of the journey there had been babies. From London to Calais, Calais to Milan, Milan to Florence. A baby had watched them from the next quartet of seats on the Inter-city. Babies had screamed and chatted and roistered and roared, been carried and rocked and coaxed and shouted at on the boat. Larger, older ones had rushed about the deck, pushed their heads over the side between the spume and the sea-gulls, all the way to France. Two Swiss six-year-old babies with the heads of financiers had been absorbed in pocket calculators across the carriage from them all the way to the frontier. The night, from Switzerland to Chiasso, had been made sleepless by the wailing of an Umbrian infant with the toothache. From Milan, the corridor had been solid with nursing mothers.

He had said, 'Evelyn, why the hell are we not travelling first class?'

'I didn't last time.'

'My heaven – nearly twenty years ago. And you were fit then. You could have just about walked to Italy then.'

'I'm fit now,' she said. 'A miscarriage isn't an illness. It's usual. A blessing. We know it.'

He was a doctor. That her miscarriage of a child was a blessing was a fact that he had levelly insisted upon since it happened, two weeks ago. The child, he had told her, had certainly been wrong. For the rest of their lives they would have been saddled with –

She had lain on the bed and said nothing. They had been married twelve years. For fifteen she had been doing medical research, as busy as he in the same teaching hospital. On her marriage she had made it clear that she had no intention of wasting herself – her youth, her training – in childbearing. Her brain was at its best. Children could come later. Good heavens, you could have a child at forty now. There was that top Civil Servant woman who had had a child – perfectly healthy child – at fifty. It had always been so – able women often produced children late. Mrs Browning – (For Evelyn was properly educated: literary as well as medical.)

And she looked so young for her age. It had become a joke at parties, how young Evelyn stayed. 'I'm Mrs Dorian Grey,' she said, though few of Mick's colleagues knew what she meant. Mick had loved her first (it sounded crude) because of her health – her health, energy and bright eyes and shiny seaside hair and out-spoken Yorkshire good sense. In a rare moment of imagination – it had made up her mind to him – he had called her 'The Scarborough Girl'. It had been her lovely, apparently indestructable youth and health and sense that had given him the courage to tell her at once after the miscarriage – directly after his consultation with her gynaecologist – that, at her age, there must be no more. To conceive a child again must be out of the question.

'Why?'

He told her. She listened thoughtfully, with a careful, consulting-room expression, not looking at him but at the waving top of the silver birch outside their bedroom window, for the miscarriage had taken place at home as they had so dashingly planned that the birth should do. The foetus had been between four and five months old. It had lain with her for an hour in the bed. It had had small limp arms. There was no telephone by the bed and she had waited an hour for him to get back from the hospital. The only sound in the empty house had been the whimpering and scratching of the dog at the bedroom door and her terrified, thumping heart fearing that it might get in. She had bled a good deal and had watched the birch tree turn its topmost leaves first one way and then the other in the evening light, had fainted as Mick arrived. As she fainted she had seemed to see his eyes in a band of brightness, separate from his face and filled with raw dismay. Afterwards – he had been so steady – she thought that this must have been a dream.

'I'm sorry,' he said now, 'I didn't know this place was opposite the Innocenti baby place. You should have let me book a good hotel. Just because you were here before –. It's no good trying to live things over again.'

'I don't try. It's lovely here. I knew it would still be lovely, even with all the traffic now. When I was here before, the piazza used to be almost empty. In the early morning there'd be just one donkey and cart going across, and someone spreading out a flower stall round the feet of the statue. Now this huge great car park. But the light's the same. And the buildings – the columns of the orphanage.'

'Come and have dinner.'

'And along here,' she said, walking ahead of him down the narrow corridor with the old slit windows, 'the floor used to crackle with the heat as if the boards were on fire.

And you could see mountainous great cedars – look. See them. Look. And just the top of the dome where the Michelangelo David is. Look how solid the trees are.'

'Oh – and the dining room's exactly the same. Exactly. Look. Pure E. M. Forster. There's even the same long table down the middle.'

They were shown, however, past the long table to one of the empty side tables. The long table, though fully laid, stayed empty.

'I was here twenty years ago,' she said to the waitress – who exclaimed and rejoiced. Afterwards Evelyn must come and see the old Signora – the very old Signora now. *At once* the girl would go and tell her. The old Signora loved people to return.

'I was still a student,' Evelyn told her as she came with the soup, 'under twenty. Oh, it was wonderful to have free wine put on the table, just like a water-jug. We hardly drank wine in England then.'

'You speak beautiful Italian,' said the waitress. 'Students have been coming here and learning good Italian, the old Signora says, for a hundred years. When were you here? Ha!' (she clapped her hands) 'Then I was the baby in the kitchen. Now' (she stroked her stomach) 'soon there shall be another baby in the kitchen.'

'I'd like to be at the long table,' said Evelyn over the pasta, which seemed very plain.

'Nobody's sitting there.'

'Everyone used to sit there. All together. Like in *A Room with a View*. D'you think we could ask? Nobody's sitting there.'

'If nobody's sitting there we might as well stay over here by the window.'

'No – if we sat there, then other people would come. We could talk. Oh Mick – I wore such a dress. Tartan taffeta! Can you imagine? I thought you had to change for dinner, you see. I'd never been anywhere. Just read Forster and Henry James. All the others were in beads and rags. It was the new fashion – rags. I hadn't met it. I was terribly behind the times.'

'This wasn't the time when you were with The Love of your Life?'

'No. I told you. It was just after Finals. Waiting for the results. I was with a girl who was chucking Medicine and going to be a nun. She went into a nunnery as soon as we got home. It was her last holiday.'

'Must have been a jolly little outing.'

'Mick'— Her laughter warmed him more than the eye-watering wine. He leaned across and took her hand. 'I'm glad you didn't go into a nunnery,' he said.

'Oh, I was pretty boring. I hadn't even got hooked on Medicine then. I only wanted everyday sort of things.'

*

The door of the dining room opened and an English family – mother, father and five children – filed in and sat at the long table. The older children folded their hands. The younger ones sat still and good. The youngest, a girl about seven, sat on her hands, her short arms stiff at each side of her until the father turned bleak wire spectacles on her and said, 'Elizabeth.' Then she took her hands from under her thighs and folded them in her lap like the rest, but the corners of her mouth became very firm. She was unusually beautiful.

'What a beautiful child,' said Evelyn. Other people at side tables were looking too.

'Yes. Come on, love, what shall we have next?'

'No choice. It's a pensione. Osso bucco every night. I told you. Mick – just *look* at that child.'

'Yes. Let's have some more wine. Leave them be.'

'Why should I? I'm all right you know. You don't have to worry. For heaven's sake, look at them all. Aren't they beautiful?'

'The mother's not,' said Mick. 'She looks worn out.'

'Yes.' Evelyn looked vaguely, but then back at the children, especially at the child Elizabeth.

'What a father,' said Mick, seeing the glasses gleam from one child to another, then the order given for all to say Grace. Five pairs of eyes shut around him. Five pairs of hands were folded together. The wife moved spoons about the cloth.

' "For what we are about to receive," ' said the father –

'I don't believe it,' Mick said. 'They must be ghosts. I'll bet they're from Hampstead.'

The children began to drink soup which had been rather laconically slapped down by the young Signora. The child, Elizabeth, looked round as the young Signora pranced by and the young Signora tickled the top of the child's head. Again the father said, 'Elizabeth.' The mother continued to stare into space.

'Shall we go to bed now?' Evelyn was across the dining room almost before she had said it.

'Aren't we going out?' He hurried after her. 'For a walk? See the Duomo and all that? I think they floodlight it. It's too early to sleep.'

'No. You go and see it if you like. I'm tired. We'll be out all day after this – every day from tomorrow morning. When Rupert comes there'll be no cloister left untrod.' Her face had lengthened and her eyes looked tired.

*

In his bed across the room from her he said, 'You're not sorry we came? It's a busy place for a convalescence.' He was staring at their painted ceiling, shadowy with carved angels.

She said, 'I remember this ceiling. D'you know, I think we were in this same room. I wonder if – the girl who became a nun, goodness, I've forgotten her name – I wonder if she remembers this ceiling.'

'You're not sorry, Evelyn? It maybe has been a bit soon.'

'Don't be a fool. God – *children* have miscarriages these days. Abortions, abortions – you hear of nothing else. A clinical fact of life now. Unless you're a Catholic. Even Catholics aren't what they were. Catholic *doctors* now are doing abortions in Africa. In the famine places. It's a rational matter.'

They both thought of the abortion reform posters they had passed, slapped over ancient buildings – church walls, palazzos – and modern banks and municipal offices, on the way from the station.

'Not my line of business, thank goodness.'

'Well, no – nor mine.'

'You're not trying to persuade yourself,' he said, 'that this is the same? This was no *choice* for heaven's sake.'

After a time, as the old wooden room cooled and crackled in the early night she said, 'No.' Then, 'What do they mean – choice?'

*

Rupert's arrival was like a salt breeze. He bounced into the mahogany and plush entrance hall, arms astretch and talking, before the young Signora had finished opening the inner door for him. He was fresh from Cyprus – the archetypal, unwed, ageless English academic, rich, Greece-loving, sexless – all passions channelled into deep concern for friends: the man you meet at college who turns up about every five years looking exactly the same and remembering every last thing about you and telling you nothing of himself. One's lynch-pin, one's strong rock. 'My dears – dears! Out. Out. Out we go at once before we're eaten by the aspidistras.' He wrapped Evelyn in his arms, gazed adoringly at the smiling young Signora over her shoulder and grabbed hold of Mick's arm. Like many men with secret lives he touched people often and bravely, hating it.

'What a place you've found. Is it real? I saw a troupe of little Nesbitts making for the Boboli Gardens with hoops and kites – a neurotic Mama and a father from the Iffley Road.

'We think Hampstead.'

'My dears – Oxford. They can only be Oxford. Mum is a lecturer in – let's see – Thermo-Dynamics and Pa is – Pa is – ha! He is a Biologist. He reads Peter Rabbit at home and picks apart little pussy cats in the day-time. He glares down microscopes at the death agonies of gnats. One day the children will all silently pack their bags and away to California. And Mama will take a tiny pistol out of her poche and shoot him through the head.'

'You know them, Rupert?'

The three of them were clattering down the pensione's stone stairs under the vaulted archway to the piazza.

'But dozens of them. Whole families of them.'

'Oxford rather than Cambridge?'

'Oh – masses more of them at Cambridge. Cousins and cousins. But in Cambridge, dears, they don't dress their children in Greenaway-yallery. It's filthy tee shirts and shaven heads. All reading Stendhal at six. Shall I tell you what happened to me last time I went to Cambridge?' He was sweeping them along the Via Servi. The crowds smiled at him, parting before him. 'Drinks,' he said, 'with a Fellow of Queen's. Sitting there talking (Coffee? Coffee? Let's stop here.) – oh, post-structuralism, Japanese realist fiction, usual stuff. Out from behind a sofa comes youngest child wearing nappies and smoking a cigarette.'

'Pot?' said Mick.

'No no no – Russian Sobranie. Twenties stuff.'

Evelyn was laughing. 'You made that up, Rupert.'

She sat back at the café table, looked at the small coffee cups, the glasses of water, the sugar lumps wrapped in paper decorated with little pictures of Raphael's Virgin and Child. She lifted her face to the sun.

'Come on Rupert, you did,' said Mick. 'These children were History Man children. University of E.A.'

'Certainly not, dear. History Man children have nothing to do with Oxford. Nowadays they're churchgoers – 1662. Learning their Collect for the day. The parents toy with communities – not communes, communities. Firmly, firmly in their own beds most of the time. If not it's away to the confessional and deep discussions over an evening milk drink. All terribly sweet. The children terribly ugly.'

Evelyn became still. She watched the sugar lump as the coffee turned it amber. 'Those pensione children weren't ugly.'

Rupert began to talk of Giotto saints and San Miniato, all of which he said if they hurried they could see before lunch. Evelyn wondered what he and Mick had said when Mick had telephoned Cyprus last week to say that their holiday together was now going to be a convalescence. Rupert stood right outside this area of loss, outside all areas of marriage. On Rupert's part the conversation would have been no more than a quick exclamation of regret – then details of his time of arrival.

Yet, as the days passed, it seemed odd how skilful Rupert was being at making Evelyn smile, in directing her away from precipices. As Mick stood vague before the Michelangelos, Rupert kept at Evelyn's side. While Mick made no plans, Rupert had pages marked each day in maps and guide books. It was Rupert who saw to it ('My dears, this is a holiday – not a *penance*') that they ate all their meals away from the pensione except for breakfast which they ate alone in their bedrooms. The admirable English family faded as if they had been the miasma they had looked.

*

On Rupert's last day, in the woods above Fiesole, they picnicked and talked and sunbathed and slept and Evelyn awoke feeling brisk and well. In her old, incisive mood she talked of packing and, back in Florence, Rupert even allowed her to do some of this for him. He smiled at her with love as they all three struggled through the screaming rush-hour traffic to the railway station in one of the painted, horse-drawn carriages he had insisted upon.

'Dotty things,' said Evelyn. '*Sentimental*, Rupert.' When she had been here before they had been the only sort of taxi. It had been different then. Pretty. Romantic. But now they were going to miss the train. Times change. You have to face reality.

'Don't you, Rupert dear?'

'No,' said Rupert, kissing her, waving goodbye, scattering largesse to porters, leaping the train as it began to move out. 'Not all at once at any rate,' he called. 'Give it time. Let it face you.'

*

It was quiet without him that evening. They were tired and the pensione was dark and still and nearly empty. The long centre table was no longer made up and they sat in their alcove with only one old lady, bent like a leaf over her library book, at another. The food was a little less staid than on their first night, the wine kinder, the noise of the traffic less disturbing. There had been one of the frequent Florentine power cuts and the stately young Signora had placed a candle inside a bell of glass on each table so that shadows made the white-washed walls serene. Evelyn and Mick sat long over their coffee. The old lady closed her book and crept away.

Then the door opened and the English family, very slightly flushed in the face, swept steadily in like a river and sat down at the long table without a word. The young Signora, coming through to remove the old lady's plate and blow out her candle, stopped and gasped. It was past nine o'clock. Over two hours late. It was as clear as if the Signora had shouted it that the kitchen was empty, the cook abed, the ovens cold. She said nothing, stood still, then after a pause went away and the family sat staring straight ahead. After quite a few minutes the Signora returned and asked, with a catch in her voice, whether they would take soup.

'Please,' said the father, candlelight on his glasses.

In the considerable time that then passed, the father said once, 'Is something wrong?' and nobody answered him.

Soup came. The Signora could manage no smile. She did not even look at the child, Elizabeth. She handed the basket of bread to each of them and, turning her big body about, disappeared through the door with head high. 'Shall we go?' said Mick to Evelyn, who was looking all the time at the child, but Evelyn said, 'No. No. Wait please.'

'Oh, Evelyn.'

'No. Just wait a bit longer. Please.'

From the shadows of the centre table somebody suddenly said very high and clear, 'The soup is cold.' The mother pushed hers away.

'I think,' said the father, 'that it must nevertheless be drunk, don't you?'

Two or three of the children put down their spoons. Elizabeth went on with the soup until it was finished.

'Shall we all finish the soup?' asked the father slowly, turning his head about. The children one by one picked up their spoons again, getting the soup down somehow with the help of the hard bread. The mother turned sideways and looked at the floor.

'Come along now, Elizabeth, eat your bread.'

'I have drunk the soup,' said Elizabeth, 'but the bread is too hard.'

'Then we shall hope that you can eat it later, shall we not?'

Pasta came, freshly made, the Signora hot in the face. Evelyn and Mick asked for more coffee and the Signora, serving it, suddenly blazed her eyes at Evelyn and poured forth a whispered torrent of Italian with backward movements of the head at the centre table. Evelyn nodded but did not take her eyes from the child.

'We shall not take meat or fruit,' said the father, 'we shall go to bed. "For what we have received —" Elizabeth?'

She did not look up.

'You have not eaten the bread.'

'It's too hard. I drank the soup.'

'Come along. Eat the bread.'

She did not move.

' "For what we have received the Lord make us truly thankful." Come along. We shall go. And Elizabeth shall stay here until she has eaten the bread.'

They went out, one of the older boys giving Elizabeth a push in the back with a friendly finger, but nobody else paid any attention, the mother leaving the room first without a glance. All their feet could be heard receding down the corridor, crackling like a forest fire, and doors were heard to close.

Suddenly, all the electricity in the pensione came on in a flood and the child was revealed like a prisoner under a search-light, all alone at the long table. She sat stalwartly, with small, round, folded arms, looking at her hands, her mouth dogged, the bread untouched on the tired cloth.

'Shall we go now?' asked Mick, loudly and cheerfully, coughing a little, squeaking back his chair.

'No. No. Not yet. I want some more coffee.'

'We can't have *more* coffee, it's much too late.'

The Signora came in again and stopped to see the child sitting alone in the glare. She turned astonished eyes on Evelyn and Mick and started towards the centre table, but the dark, fierce air hanging around the child made her shy.

'You – finito? Everyone now?'

The child did not answer.

'Could we have more coffee? I'm sorry – I know it's terribly late,' called Evelyn and looking back over her shoulder at the child all the way to the door, the Signora made for the kitchen again.

Mick began to hum and pace the floor a little. He looked out of the window where the colonnade of the Innocenti blazed patchily above the whirling lights of the cars. Above was the starry sky. Turning in to the room again, he said, 'Hard old bread, isn't it?' and went and sat down by the child. 'Enjoying your holiday?' he said. 'Expect it's all a bit of a bore, isn't it? Churches and stuff. I expect you'd rather be at the sea.'

Then he put out his hand and let it stay for a moment above the child's head. He let it drop and began slowly to stroke her hair. She flung up her chin and pulled away as though she had been stung and simultaneously the door to the corridor opened and the father stood in the dining room. He said, 'What is this?'

'I was talking to your daughter.'

'I'm afraid my daughter is not allowed to talk to strangers.'

'Isn't it rather unwise then to let her sit alone, long after her bedtime, in a room with only strangers in it?'

'She knows how to behave. She knows that she has to stay there until she has eaten the bread.'

'That's your affair –'

'It is.'

'It's your affair, but suppose that the strangers had not been us? To leave a small child alone. Late at night. In a foreign restaurant.'

'Hardly a restaurant I think.'

'You treated it as a restaurant tonight. Over two hours late for dinner. Never a word of apology. The one and only waitress tired out. Pregnant. Behaving like lord and peasant – I'm sorry. I'm sorry, but my wife and I have been horrified. Disgusted. Disgusted with you. Never seen such idiocy. Quaint. Victorian play-acting. You need a psychiatrist – not fit to have children.'

'Are you an authority on children?'

'I – yes. I am a doctor. I know a lot about children.'

'And how many have you?'

'That's not the point. I see a child being studiously, insanely –'

'Shall we continue this outside?'

'By all means. If you will send this child at once to bed.'

'I shall consider it when we have talked. Outside this room if you please. I don't believe in discussions of this sort in front of children.'

'Very well.'

As the father swung out of the room and Mick swung after him, Evelyn saw in her husband's eyes the remote, terrible band of dismay she thought she had dreamt before. He was blind to her. She put her head in her hands and thought, 'I never knew. In all the years, I never asked. I never knew. I never thought of him.'

Lifting her face, she found that the little girl was looking at her with interest. The bread was still uneaten on the cloth. Her face was serious. She said to Evelyn, 'Don't cry. It doesn't matter.'

'I'm not. I wasn't –'

'It was a puncture. We got late. He's terribly ashamed. It's all right.'

'I – I just didn't –'

Tramping feet, loud voices were to be heard returning and the child, looking kindly still at Evelyn, sighed and picked up the bread in both fists.

'Oh no – oh no! Please don't,' cried Evelyn. 'Please let me have it – please. I'll hide it in my bag.' She held out her arms. 'Throw it me. Throw it me.'

But Elizabeth, shocked, turned away. 'It's all *right*,' she said, and began to munch.

The two men as they returned, saw first this loyal munching and then Evelyn in her corner, weeping at last.

The Pig Boy

Veronica smelled the pig boy before she saw him and the smell was the essence of her loathing and hatred of Hong Kong.

A wet, grey, bad-tempered, blowy day and cold. She was wearing a new warm jersey under her white summer suit. Back at the hotel were all the thin summer clothes she had brought with her, still unworn. She had felt the room-boy's disdain as he unpacked them. Here was a first-time-out wife. She didn't know a thing. Didn't know that as late as March it could be cold and wet and bleak. Colder than England.

Colder than Barnes, she thought. She had left London with the grass on Barnes Common brightening and long and all the candles shining on the avenue of chestnuts that crosses the pretty railway line. London had had the smell of summer – airy and fresh. Here there was grit in the air and rubbish blew about the streets like rags.

Her husband was at work. He would be at work tonight until eight o'clock. Then there would be the usual drinks party. Perhaps two parties. Then the usual meal in a restaurant with friends. Then the usual wander in the streets among the stalls. Then bed. At the weekend – her last weekend – the firm had offered them a hired car.

But it wasn't being much of a holiday, alone all day. Well, of course it was not meant to be holiday. She was just there. There as a wife. A brought-out wife, paid for by Geoffrey's firm. She was to be brought-out (tourist class) every six months for a few weeks until he finished the job. Like most other wives with husbands working abroad she was safety-valve procedure against executive breakdown.

The air must be full of flying wives, thought Veronica – airlines to Singapore, Hong Kong, the Philippines, Colombo heavy with wives flying husbandwards: oil wives, lawyers' wives, army wives – complacent on the journey out, glum or tense or relieved on the flight home again, leaving their husbands not necessarily to any great amusement. Geoffrey had said, 'Look round. Look at all the men sitting eating alone. Not exactly the glossy life, is it?' 'Yes – my wife's at home,' said the husbands. 'No – well she can't really. Children's education.' Or, 'No. She can't. She has her job. No, it's not much fun, but it's not forever. You learn to manage.'

And the world was full of people pitying the wives, thought Veronica. In Barnes the drinks parties glittered with sharp eyes – if you were lucky enough to be invited to any without a man. 'Yes, I'm married,' you said, 'my husband's working in Hong Kong. Oh yes – but I do get out there you know. Several weeks twice a year.'

'That sounds terrible.'

'It's very usual. Very usual nowadays. After all, it's not new. Look at army wives and sailors' wives – they've always done it. One's independent after all.'

'Not much fun though.'

'Oh, I don't know.'

The guarded look behind the eyes which said, 'Is she faithful? I'll bet she's not. I'll bet he's not either. Asking too much – alone six months of the year.'

Then would come the invitation – or no invitation. Whichever happened, it was insulting.

And for Veronica, even in the liberated streets of Barnes, staying at home was harder to explain than for many because she had no children. Being a painter she could have worked anywhere.

'No – we have no children.'

'Don't you think of being with him then?'

'Oh – I think I'd hate Hong Kong. And there are things here I can't really leave.'

'What is it she can't leave?' they thought. 'She's probably

just found that she could never really stand him. There's probably trouble. I wonder what her lover's like?'

But there was no lover and there had never been trouble, and it was a surprise to find that when she arrived in Hong Kong this first time she found herself thinking, 'What if he's changed? What if I don't like him?' Dazed still by the idiot film she had watched on the flight and a couple of magazines the woman sitting next to her had loaned her, she thought, 'I wonder what his woman's like? Chinese? They're very pretty. Doting, too. Everyone will know about her except me. They'll think nothing of it. It's the custom of the job, the times. Probably always was. Insane to be chaste. I wonder why I am?'

'I don't want to see him,' she thought, waiting for her luggage to lumber up on the roundabout. 'I'm frightened.' The roundabout went hypnotically, smoothly round, black and quiet like a roulette wheel. The Englishwoman with the magazines came up to her looking fuzzy and excited – little suit and brooches. 'Forget – did you say you were army? Are you an army wife? Are you going to the married quarters?'

'No I'm not.' Suddenly angry, Veronica said, 'I work. I do a job.'

'Oh,' said the woman eyeing her, unbelieving. 'I thought if he wasn't here to meet you we could share a taxi.'

'I'm staying at the Peninsula.'

'Oh my! I'm sorry.' She looked hard at Veronica, not believing that a woman she had seen looking so uncertain could be staying at the Peninsula, though – Geoffrey had let his flat and was spendthrifting weeks of pay – this was true. They went through Customs together. An aggressive Chinese man–woman in police-type uniform shouted at them and glared. It was cold and the wind whined.

'I hadn't expected this,' said Veronica.

'First time out then?' The woman perked up.

'Yes.'

'Oh – you'll love it. I've been out five times. Lovely shopping.'

And there was Geoffrey, a tireder looking Geoffrey, rather redder in the face and flabbier, his shirt bloused out a bit over his trousers, but his eyes bright. Looking for her.

At once all thoughts of mistresses and lovers became ridiculous, their recognition of each other complete. Hurtling in the taxi through up-and-down rivers of lights, they held tight to each other's hand, and all the old pleasures flowed back.

It was the day time without him that had become so deadly boring. She felt so ashamed – the first time in the East – to be bored.

Geoffrey got up at seven-thirty and they had breakfast in their room – a great trolley wheeled in by two waiters, like an old film. The trolley had huge silver dish-covers, omelettes, mountains of croissants, huge pots of coffee, a pyramid of butter (which Geoffrey because of the blousing out of the shirt did not eat. 'Chinese call it cow's grease. Puts you off. Convenient.'). And there were shiny cloth napkins the same colour as the cloth and fresh flowers in a glass.

When he had gone to work she would dress slowly and wander about. Then she would go down in the lift with its bowing attendant and leave the room-key in the lobby. Then she would walk purposefully out of the great white and gold hall into the street and let the crowd sweep her along.

For the first days, just to be in the marching streets was something, being swept up with the rest into a whirlpool at traffic lights, then like water, surging across. She crossed to Hong Kong Side and the crowds at the ferries nearly trampled her under. She loved this at first. It was like going out further from the shore where the bigger waves might knock you down and bear you away and nobody know.

But after a week or so she grew used to it – used to the pace and the impersonality. It was just a richer, madder Oxford Street on a Saturday afternoon. She began to notice a pair of shoes in a display window in the side of the Peninsula hotel. Two hundred pounds. The first day the price of the shoes had seemed ludicrous. After a week or so of Hong Kong it seemed just the price of shoes.

She grew used to the legless woman who shuffled her way about the pavement under the shoes, and around the corner, among the little clutch of street stalls that appeared by magic every morning. People stepped over the woman as if she were a moving sack. Food from the stalls dropped on her as she held up her tin cup for money. 'She has to pay for that pitch,' said a lawyer friend of Geoffrey, 'like the door-man at Claridges.'

Veronica got used to the Hakkar gypsy woman with the two-year-old squatting beside her and the sharp professional gypsy wag of the head as she sent the child running after her down Nathan Road to pull at her skirt. 'Money, money, money,' the child said – angrily, like the Customs official. Its mouth was covered in sores. She grew used to this.

One day she took the harbour cruise and sat in a cold greenhouse of a boat to see the city from the sea. The lunatic, concrete growths stuck up in a forest of sharp-edged temples. They looked pushed into holes in the hills, and at their feet, among the dark little tents of the squatters was the noise of more cranes, more drills, more bulldozers, tearing away, knocking down, building yet more. It seemed like no country.

Another day she took a taxi and watched the boat families at Aberdeen from another glass greenhouse. She watched the chickens and babies and birds in cages on the decks and the screaming women in huge shields of hats all tipping and tossing over the choppy cold waves. All looked an exhibition, put on for the brought-out wives. It was not real. She was bored.

Lunch somewhere, if she remembered, and then back to the hotel for a rest (a rest from what? She was twenty-five, healthy and a full-time painter), then maybe an invitation from one of the resident wives to go shopping. They might be Chinese or French or American or English, but the conversation was always the same. Then the noisy, boozy, sociable evening in the glaring streets with Geoffrey and friends. All in the streets at night was self-consciously wicked – the transvestite street, the blue-film and massage-shop street, the nude-photograph street. Thousands of tourists.

And she was bored.

It might have been Soho except for the crazy zig-zag glitter of the lights – soft yellow and pink and gold and white and green. 'It's the pale green ones that make it Chinese,' said Geoffrey. 'The rest could be anywhere – though nowhere so many. I love the pale green.'

It was the first time he had said that he loved something here.

'D'you not long for proper green?' she said. 'You said you did. In letters.'

'Proper green?'

'You said you'd started watching television just for the scenery. Watching Westerns to see the grass.'

'Oh – there's grass here if you look. Up in the New Territories grass all the way to China. You can walk for miles. We'll go at the weekend in the car. And there's green on the islands. It's wonderfully beautiful. You can sunbathe on Cheung Chau. Next time you come out it will be really hot.'

'I think you're beginning to like it.'

'Oh – yes. What?' He was watching five little boys spooning what looked like baby snakes into their mouths from blue and white egg-cups. The naked light-bulbs over the stalls swung in the wind. They looked like Christmas tree fruits. They made shadows come and go across the five pale faces. Hair shone like tar.

'You aren't beginning to want to stay? I mean *stay*? Not go home – stay here permanently?'

'God no,' he said, 'I'm here for quick money like everyone else. You know that. We can earn more here in six months than in ten years at home. It's why we did it. Hell!'

They walked back through the packed midnight. The tenement walls hung above the narrow streets like the flanks of galleons, dressed over-all, night and day, with long poles of washing. From the lamp-lit rooms behind came the soft shuffling knock of the mah-jong games, floating out over the night until it was part of the night, like cicadas in Italy.

*

So now, towards the end, Geoffrey had an all-day meeting and would not be in until after eight o'clock and Veronica was to have lunch with the wife of his boss – an English-woman from Kent who had come out to live in Hong Kong permanently. She and the wife would then go shopping for silk and perhaps some jewellery which the wife would advise about and get good discount. Veronica took a taxi from the Hong Kong side ferry and it wound up the Peak, round flower beds and gardens. But cement piles were going up even among these. A shining building that looked scarcely finished was being pulled down again to make way for something more modern. A speeded-up film of the building of Hong Kong thought Veronica, would be like the waves of the sea, rising and breaking to rise again. The gardens were certainly doomed, she thought. However much must this land be worth? The Cathedral must be sitting on a fortune. A thousand pounds a centimetre. Ten thousand pounds a geranium.

The taxi swung off the road into a tunnel of expensive white tiles and cork-screwed up it to a double meshed door. A servant in a long black dress answered it – hair screwed back, waxed yellow face, tight cheek-bones, greying hair and a sweet smile. She seemed uncertain though about letting Veronica in and disappeared for quite some time. Veronica stood in the windy tunnel.

Then down in a flurry came the lady from Kent, by no means so flawlessly dressed as at the party where Veronica had met her. Her hair flopped about. The finger nails of one hand were painted and held a brush for the fingers of the other hand which were still plain. She embraced Veronica wildly with both arms. Veronica hoped the lacquer wasn't spilling down her back.

'My dear! But it's terrible! I'd forgotten.'

'It doesn't matter at all.'

'Sit down. A drink. Oh but this is awful. I've never done it before. That party – so noisy. I do this. I *throw* invitations about. But I've never, never forgotten. Ever. I could die.'

'It's quite all right.' Veronica wondered why she couldn't just stay. 'There's heaps I can do instead.'

'Are you here for a nice long time?'

'Another week.'

'Look, I'll get the diary. We'll fix something now. Wednesday – no, I can't do Wednesday. Say Friday and I'll cancel my hair. Or Sunday – what about this Sunday and Geoffrey can come too?'

'We were – hoping for a car this weekend. To go to the New Territories.'

'Oh dear, well Monday then?'

'I'll be gone by Monday. Look – don't worry. It's nice to be here now. Nice to come for a drink.'

'You see I have a Bridge.'

Veronica thought for a moment of teeth. Perhaps new teeth making lunch difficult.

'A Bridge – the wife of – well, it's a Royal Command sort of thing. There are two tables – a French table and an Anglo-Chinese table. And tea. Look – do you play Bridge?'

'No I'm afraid –'

'Of course not. You work, don't you?'

'I'm a painter.'

'Oh, a *painter*. Oh wonderful. I'm sure there are a lot of painters in Hong Kong. Well, I believe there's a wife at Jardines – does Chinese heads. Makes quite a little business of – Look, why don't I take you to the Bridge? It'd be quite an experience for you. It's quite serious stuff you know. It might amuse – It's *real* Bridge.'

'No, no –'

But the woman had decided. She was stretching for the jade green telephone and talking ten to the dozen. They ate some biscuits and drank some more gin.

'You don't want to bother with lunch, do you? The food here is the big danger. We get as greedy as the Chinese. Aren't you loving the restaurants?'

'Yes, loving them.'

'I hope Geoffrey's doing you proud? We hardly see him. I hear he's moved to the Pen. with you?'

'Yes.'

'Oh, *rather* fun.'

A taxi took them to a house even higher up the Peak –

servants, glass, marble floors, rare pieces of curly black ebony and small figurines of jade. The French table was already under weigh – tight mouths, severe hair-cuts, fast conversation. The sharp faces on the cards looked back. The Chinese/English table was more relaxed except at moments when a deep silence fell and eyes became filled with intent. Veronica sat apart on a silk sofa beside a silk screen and watched the rings shining on the confident international fingers. Outside the window birds tipped and soared on the cold wind.

An older, Chinese woman came across to Veronica when tea was brought and sat by her. She said, in a Knightsbridge voice, 'How are you liking Hong Kong? I believe it is your first time?

'Oh very much. Yes, it is.'

'You are from London?'

'Yes. From Barnes.'

'Ah – from Barnes.'

A louder Chinese lady came across. She had round red spots painted on her cheeks and corkscrew curls. She spoke in a high, rather cockney sing-song.

'You will be going to London soon? Then you must stay in my flat. In Ken Sing Tong.'

'But I live in –'

'You like Hong Kong?'

'Oh, yes, very –'

Little cakes made of chestnut purée wrapped in pale green marzipan were handed with the tea. The purée was piped in little worms like the things the boys were eating at the street stalls. The pale green marzipan was like the green of the neon. 'The pale green that is Chinese.'

'But it isn't,' thought Veronica. 'It is just pale green. I've seen those cakes in Fortnums, just as, come to think of it, I've seen that queer stuff on the street stalls. It was noodles. This place isn't any more foreign than London. None of it.'

The lady who had offered her a flat in Kensington took three little cakes, ate them greedily and licked her painted fingers heavy with diamonds.

'Nothing Chinese here,' thought Veronica, looking at

all the ebony and jade and silk and the Chinese carpet on the floor. 'It is the Finchley Road.'

'I am hating it,' she thought, and got up.

'I must go,' she said. The women were going back to the tables. 'Oh dear,' said the Boss's wife. 'Oh hell – I did bish it up didn't I? Must you go?'

'I must, I'm afraid. I'm meeting someone Kowloon Side.'

It was the most inconvenient moment to leave and she knew it. The hostess was trying to get the tables back together again against a lot of fast talking by the French in corners. Servants were gliding about trying to gather unobtrusively the remains of the tea. 'So glad you could come,' said the hostess with a far-away calm that did not disguise her alertness to developments in more significant parts of the room. 'We'll meet again – won't we?' said the Boss's wife. 'We've all so wondered what dear Geoffrey's wife would be like.'

Two of the French women stopped talking then and looked at Veronica quickly.

Looking round, Veronica thought, 'They are all devious. Every one of them. What are they really thinking about behind all the witty talk and the picking up of the cards and the laying down of them?' Laughter followed her out of the room and she thought that it did not sound very kind. I liked the noise of the mah-jong players better than that, she thought. Getting off the ferry Kowloon Side, it was still not five o'clock. Over three hours to go. She had not a thing to do.

*

When she reached the Peninsula she found that she could not go in. She walked instead along the side of it, past the little inset shop windows and the two hundred pound shoes. She thought of the rings and the earrings and the even more beautiful shoes of the women playing cards on the Peak. As she stood a woman passed her, bouncing and busty. She was coming from a hairdresser, the hair raised up in a cushion, stiff with lacquer. She was the woman from the aeroplane, the army wife. She walked jauntily past Veronica, not recognising her. It might be Barnes, thought Veronica, or Ken Sing Tong.

Then she found that she was walking away and away from the hotel and away and away down Nathan Road. At first she walked quite slowly, but then she began to walk fast, watching for the traffic, but beginning to walk in and out of it. She began to march at the same quick, steady pace as everyone else in the crowded street.

And soon she found that she was caught up with the people on the pavement. She was in a marching army. Nobody looked at her, touched her, jostled her. Nobody in the street ever seemed to touch anybody else. And they made way for you without noticing you. You began to melt through the crowd like a spirit. There were no collisions. It was like radar, like bats. Up on their toes they all walked, their faces looking straight ahead, their arms to their sides. Perhaps, thought Veronica, if you live so closely, so densely together, you have to develop this isolation. Nobody noticed her, walking, walking, marching, marching. And, as she turned off into a side street for no real reason and marched on she realised that she had stopped being unhappy.

On a corner a minute old woman sold purple chrysanthemums and Veronica bought six. They seemed very cheap. The old woman with little yellow hands wrapped the stalks in yellow paper. Her hands were like fans. Ivory fans. They had no pictures on them. No faces.

'I think I'm a bit mad,' said Veronica. 'What shall I do with these flowers?'

The wind blew and it began to rain. The rain was cold on her face and the paper round the flowers grew sopped and useless. She let it float away into the gutter with other rubbish, and walked on.

'I think I must be hungry,' she said, 'I ought to have eaten some of those Mr Kipling chestnut things. I'll find a street stall. Geoffrey said, "Never a street stall. Never in Hong Kong," he said. "Singapore yes. Hong Kong never. Look at the pots they cook in. Slopped round with a greasy cloth. Never washed up." '

'I'll eat at a street stall,' she said.

But there seemed now to be no stalls. She had walked since leaving Nathan Road down a dozen small streets and got back to a main road again – dirtier and greyer with only a faint glitter from the tram lines and overhead wires tossing with rain and wind. Traffic screamed by. The people thinned. The trams and buses were packed with those going home from work and other thousands arriving for the evening shift. She didn't know whether to try and cross this road or not, and realised she was quite lost. Also, it seemed – but this must surely be because there was a storm coming – to be getting quite dark.

Then she was out of the street and on a great motorway, a huge clover-leaf junction. The crowd had disappeared and there was no one about. Only traffic – mostly big square lorries – streamed by. It was an enormously wide road, two triple carriageways and a scruffy central reservation. At the far side there seemed to be grass and a large, low, sad-looking building, a sort of club house. Maybe she could get a taxi back from there?

All alone in the ridiculous white suit she ran from the edge of the motorway to the central reservation and stood there between the whizzing lorries, waiting for the second dash to the far shore. And there she smelled the pig boy.

He was in a lorry – a lorry still far away up the road, but the smell was so huge and terrible that she looked about her, up and down the road, to see if some great sewer were leaking near her feet. The wind then carried the smell in a blast into her mouth so that she retched and dropped the flowers and pressed her hands over her face. Her eyes streamed with water. She struggled to get her handkerchief – anything – out of her bag, and with a clashing, cranking roar the lorry came up beside her.

The back of it was filled to the brim with screaming pigs – dark with dirt, tossed in a writhing mass, suffering, fighting with pathetic, inadequate feet to get somehow steady and in control of their great bodies. The pigs at the bottom of the heap – their gaping faces pressed into the slats – seemed already dead.

But it was the smell. It made her nearly faint.

'You want help?'

It was the driver. The pig boy. High above her head he looked down. She turned away sick, 'No, no.'

'You lost? English? You want help?'

He was not Chinese like the flower-seller, or the servants on the Peak, or the ivory-carved room-boys at the hotel, or even the red faced Hakkar professional beggar. He had a broad face, laughing cheek-bones, long, bright Mongolian eyes and curly hair.

'Thanks,' she gasped. 'No. It's fine, thanks. I'm just going – over there. To get a taxi.'

'That place shut there now over there. That place shut. For new building. Re-settlement. Old English tennis club. Nobody now. Where you stay?'

'The Peninsula.'

'Four-five mile soon dark.'

'It's all right. Please go.' She – still nearly fainting – tried to cross the road behind the lorry.

But he had jumped down and came towards her. He took her wrist and pulled her to the front of the lorry and tumbled her up and in. She retched again and her forehead fell down against the dashboard.

'You ill?' He had started the engine though it could hardly be heard against the screaming of the pigs. He turned on the radio. Chinese music wailed through the cab, too.

'The smell, the smell!'

'Oh, *smell*,' he said and began to laugh. 'Terrible, terrible smell.' He laughed with his eyes and his shoulders and his mouth and with every bit of him. Clusters of good luck charms hung across the windscreen of the cab – tokens, ribbons, silly animals dangling from strings, and several photographs of girls. Veronica turned from all of them and leaned her head against the rattling, vibrating door. 'Terrible smell!' He laughed with pride. She remembered how the room-boys had laughed and laughed, Geoffrey had told her, when he had hurt his back soon after he arrived and had had to lie down on a hard board. 'Terrible pain,' they had laughed. And someone else, telling her of a visit to a Chinese dentist – and on the Peak at that – had asked 'Is this going to hurt?' 'Oh yes – it going to hurt all right,' and had roared with laughter. Something at last was different here.

The lorry had turned off the motorway and down a drab road, seeming to turn away from the Centre again. It rattled past warehouses and long grey sheds. By one of them it stopped. Some people came out, wearing cloths across their faces. The driver jumped out and went over to them and they all went into the shed. Veronica, still holding the handkerchief to her mouth, sweating with sickness, struggled with the door but it wouldn't open from the inside. She felt utter terror now through the sickness and began to cry.

Then the door was opened and she fell out into the pig boy's arms. He jumped back at once. He looked shocked and only when he was sure she was safe on her feet did he shout above the pigs, 'Please – come with me now.'

She could think only of getting away from the hell of the lorry and as he turned she followed, out of the filthy yard, along a wire-fenced road, then down an alley that led to another alley that led to another that led to a busy road again. They walked, one behind the other along this road until they came to an iron bridge. Under the bridge were some stalls selling kites – sharp yellow and red and blue. Around them people were eating and talking and shouting and under the bridge a man was squatting in vest and underpants playing an instrument balanced with a spike like a miniature cello on the pavement. It looked like something between a guitar, a cello and a lute and the noise that came from it was like chalk drawn across a blackboard and in its way hurt like the smell of the pigs.

As Veronica watched, the musician looked up and smiled at her and the sun came out. All the coloured kites blazed for a moment in the sunset.

'Quick, quick,' said the pig boy and walked lithe and fast under the bridge and into a dark street. As they reached it, out came the sun again and Veronica saw the street crumbling before her. A lumpish, medieval machine, very different from the mechanics on the Peak, slowly swung a huge iron ball at a tall, papery old building. The whole front of the building slipped quietly to the ground and the sun went in again.

'I am being shown things,' said Veronica, 'like Faust.' They went on down the dark and filthy street. 'Or maybe I am being kidnapped. Perhaps I am about to be raped. Or knifed. Geoffrey – all of them, said, "Never go Kowloon Side alone." I am mad.' But she walked quietly on behind the pig boy.

He stopped and said, 'Tea?'

'No – no. Please – I want to go home. Can you find me a – bus or a taxi or something? I must get back.'

'You are ill. Tea first and then home.'

They were standing outside a dirty, blackened house with a very narrow, dark doorway. It was the oldest house she had seen in Hong Kong. Outside it, on two ancient basket chairs there sat an old woman and a very, very old man dressed in black tunics and black trousers. They sat very straight, like royal people. The woman looked at Veronica and bowed. The man looked gravely at her for rather longer, and then bowed. Nobody spoke, and in the quiet Veronica could still hear the piercing music of the lute player that now sounded the only right music for the scene.

Then, from across the road, next to the house that was being pulled down, people came running and gathering round a queer, high car, piled high with paper flowers – pink and red and yellow and white. They chattered and laughed and fussed and took no notice of Veronica or the ancient royal personages or the demolition.

The pig boy had disappeared, but he now came out of the dark doorway between the two basket chairs with a painted Chinese girl who looked at Veronica and smiled. From the thickness and symmetry of the paint Veronica saw that the girl was a prostitute. Several other girls came out who looked like her sisters. They seemed dolls from a box. Then someone else came and laid a cleanish sheet of white paper on the pavement and bowed to Veronica to sit on it. Then an older woman in a thick woollen suit and a gold bangle round her ankle brought a tiny bowl of tea.

Veronica drank it, and caught the eye of the old people.

The old woman smiled, showing a mouth full of gold teeth. The old gentleman touched first one side of his long moustaches and then the other before smiling, too. Across the road the wild party surged about the car, filling and covering it with more and more paper flowers. The pig boy, who had been talking to the painted girls, came over and said, 'You happy and well?'

She drank the tea.

'It is a funeral,' said the boy. 'You have come to a funeral.' He repeated this to the others in some sort of language and everyone laughed tremendously. He said, 'You are dressed in white for the funeral.' Their laughter mixed with the laughter and shouts of the funeral party across the road, as it moved off.

The sun had gone in now. The dust from the demolished building hung heavy. The pig boy stank. Rubbish was piled in the gutter. The woman brought more tea. The queer music went faintly on.

'You happy and well?'

Veronica said, 'Oh I am happy. I am well.' This was translated, and the old aristocrats bowed. There was silence.

Veronica realised sadly that they were expecting her to go. She stood up and said to the pig boy, 'I wish I had kept my flowers, my flowers to give them. I let them drop.'

This was translated and there was more bowing. Veronica shook hands with everyone. They took her hand with a very slight hesitation. Following the pig boy, she turned at the end of the road to wave to them, but there was no one on the street at all except the two old people and they seemed to be sitting thoughtfully looking in another direction.

The pig boy walked ahead and then after a while beside her, saying nothing. She could hardly keep up. He had fallen quite silent and she said, 'Please – can I get a bus or taxi now? I thought I saw a taxi just then.'

'No taxi,' he said. 'You are back hotel.'

'Where?'

'One minute now. Two minute.'

'It can't be.'

Yet the streets were different, noisier, busier. There were tourists about. Then all at once, there was the Hakkar beggar with her child, but now, the pig boy beside her, the child did not come after her crying 'Money.'

'I should tell you,' said the pig boy, 'that you must not take hands. You must not take hands here or embrace.'

'I'm sorry. I just wanted to say thank you to them.'

He walked on, filthy and beautiful and rough in the rich street. The crowd was changing every moment, growing smarter, faster, better dressed. He wove expertly among them.

'What are you? Who are you?' she said.

'A pig boy. I bring pigs every day out of Red China into Hong Kong. Chinese pigs. Big trading.'

'Yes, I see.'

'Good job,' he said. 'Sweet and sour' – he laughed. 'Only for strong men.'

'Oh goodness,' she said – here were the shoes, 'oh goodness, we're back at the Peninsula. Oh thank you, thank you.' She turned to the pig boy and not able to help it held out to him both her hands. He looked at them unsmiling.

'You took my wrist,' she said, 'to pull me into the cab.'

Briefly he touched her hands with his own and was gone.

'My God!' It was Geoffrey beside her getting out of a taxi. He carried a brief case and a pile of papers. 'You just back? You've had a long day. It's past nine. God, this bloody place. I hate it. Let's get a bath and – heavens, you smell dreadful. Wherever's the memsahib been taking you?'

'*Do* you hate it?' She could not move one step until Geoffrey had answered. If she moved she knew that something would break. 'Do you hate it here?'

'Well – no. But you do.'

'Do I?'

'You know you do. I know you do. I've known all the time.'

They stood on the pavement and the crowds washed effortlessly by. 'You couldn't live here, Veronica.'

'I might,' she said, 'I might.'

The Kiss of Life

Edna was a big respectable-looking woman, always in the supermarket. At least she always seemed to be in the supermarket when Mew went there which was three times a week. Mew lived alone and did not see many people except out shopping. The supermarket seemed to keep her in touch.

She had not a great need of food. A pot of marmalade lasted her nearly a month and she wished you could buy butter in less than half pounds, because even in a fridge butter goes off, being so old. Mew would pick up and feel and then put down again the cold, hard bricks of butter, especially far away foreign butter like New Zealand, and think of ambling herds with the morning sun on their coats rocking their heads and twitching their tails beside hot springs and wattle while Putney was fast asleep. It stood to reason that this butter must be old. As for the French soft stuff and the tasteless Dutch — Sometimes she gave herself a treat and afforded English butter. Even that had not the colour one expected.

Mew was fussy about colour and spent minutes each week regarding the supermarket fruit, like a still stone in the tide of women hurtling round her with big full trolleys, children kicking their heels in the trolley baskets, their legs like hanging plants as they wailed for sweets. It was in front of the fruit that Edna first spoke to Mew, just as Mew had picked up a peach.

'You're not meant to touch the peaches,' said large Edna, looking down severely from between her earrings and above her good British Home Stores macintosh.

'I was just smelling it,' said Mew, rather frightened and not truthful, for she had in fact been touching it, too, and been about to put it against her face to touch it more.

'It's not sanitary,' said Edna. 'It's the way colds get passed. By touch. You'll have to buy it now. You can't put it back.'

'Won't she?' she asked an assistant running by with papers on a clip-board.

'You what?'

'She'll have to buy the peach. She's touched it.'

The young man looked at Edna's big, firm face with its mouth turned into a confident, tight bunch like the top of a sponge-bag. Her hair was neatly permed. Little Mew looked wispy and scared. It was not easy to look severely at Mew but it was easier than to look severely at alarming Edna. 'Yes, you will,' he said, 'if you've got it out of the blue paper you will,' and he flapped off.

'I was going to buy it anyway,' said Mew. Edna stood for a moment. Then she gave a sharp approving nod and when Mew moved off went with her, pausing now and then to touch Mew's arm and point out special offers. At the check-out Mew was surprised to find that she had bought much more than usual and several things she did not want at all, like condensed milk.

'I can't think what I'm doing with condensed milk,' she said as she walked with Edna down the street. 'I couldn't stomach it even in the War.'

'It's amazing what you can stomach if you have to. It depends on your experiences,' said Edna. 'I happened to undergo the Blitz.'

'Yes, so did I,' Mew began to say, but Edna added, 'I lost everything – family, property, possessions. They lost all my records.'

'Records?' For a moment Mew thought of a slim, romantic young version of this strong-charactered woman searching tearfully among ashes for Bach and Haydn. Or Vera Lynn.

'Even my birth certificate they lost,' said Edna, 'I don't even get the pension.'

Mew thought that the macintosh looked quite an expensive one and that the woman looked rather young for the pension. 'I suppose you have your work?' she said.

Edna smiled kindly. She said, 'I'm afraid I've not been well enough to work for a *very* long time.' Mew found herself giving Edna the condensed milk.

After that they met up in the supermarket most days Mew was there, first for just a word or two, and then for quite nice long conversations round the delicatessen queue, or when they were browsing – just from interest – at the Gourmet Gondola.

'Isn't it funny – calling a counter a gondola?' said Mew. 'I think it's priceless really. Fancy a gondola all stacked up with chicken breasts and peaches in brandy.' Edna stared roundly at Mew, but had nothing to add.

'I mean – gondola,' said Mew. 'In a place like this.'

For a hazy second, Edna's eyes wavered into vagueness. In any other woman it was a look which you would have said meant that she felt out-classed, but all she did was take a jar of Gentleman's Relish off the shelf and hold it out to Mew and say, 'Disgusting!'

That as it happened was the day of the very embarrassing incident. As they both reached the check-out, Edna went first through and then waited for Mew who put down her basket-load on the moving, rubber mat and went to the other end of it to gather the things together into her small leather shopping bag. She opened the bag and gave a little shriek. 'Look,' she cried, 'there's four tins of tuna fish in my bag.'

The girl on the till stopped playing the keys and turned her plastic, moon face on Mew. Then she pressed a bell and a man in a good suit with a blue bar across the lapel was suddenly at Mew's side. Edna turned away and walked out of the glass doors that opened as she approached, and stood reflectively on the pavement, watching the cars go by.

'But I don't like tuna fish. I'd never buy it.'

'Who has reported this?' asked the man.

'Well, nobody. I have. I just found them. I don't know where they came from but they are certainly not mine.'

People behind her in the queue were watching, some with a little interest, some with the lethargy of those who have seen everything before. Someone said, 'Come on. Can we get on now? We're in a hurry. Do it in the office.'

'Were you with someone?' said the man.

'Not really. Just talking to –' She looked for Edna but Edna was not on the pavement any more. 'Well, there was someone I was sort of with. I don't exactly know her. Her name's Edna. She's gone.' Mew looked at the man, straight and bewildered and wretched. 'I really don't want these at all.'

'Come on now,' said the queue.

'Do I have to have them? I'll pay for them of course if I have. I could take them to a Bring-and-Buy.'

The man had a stern face, brisk grey hair, a fierce military moustache, but kind eyes. The blue bar on his lapel said, 'Mr Paterson' which was a name Mew found Scotch and comforting. 'I have Scotch blood myself,' she thought. 'We're very just,' and even in the middle of this terrible situation could not keep herself from imagining this Mr Paterson in a kilt standing justly at the head of a glen. She said, 'Oh Mr Paterson. I really have no wish for this tuna fish. I think I have been the victim of a hoax,' and Mr Paterson, glaring with venom at the drooping queue of customers and the immobile till-girl said, 'Yes. I believe you have. No – you needn't pay for them. Let me have them. And be much more careful in future.'

She heard people say as she went out, 'Lucky for some,' and, dipping her head put a handkerchief in her mouth. 'Actress, too,' said someone. Down the street – Edna was nowhere to be seen – Mew began to shake so much that she could hardly get the key into her front door. Inside it at last, she fell on the front room sofa and wept.

'But I'll go back,' she thought, 'I've done nothing wrong. I'll go back. I'll go back in all the same clothes – not disguised. I'll behave as I've always done. I like the supermarket. It's the only time I see a crowd, except on the television. You get dull, just running in and out of the end shop, let alone the prices.'

So she continued to shop as usual, quietly dignified at every gondola, behaving calmly at the check-out, saying good-afternoon to the till-girl as she had always done and because no one else seemed to. Speaking, however, to no one.

After about a month, she saw Edna again standing before the cleaning fluids. She appeared to be examining several varieties of bleach, though her wire basket was empty. The macintosh had a button off and looked rather grubby, and her shoes were very down-at-heel. Her hair was dirty. Holding the bleach close to her face, she seemed to be talking to it. Mew turned away.

But then she thought of Edna's records and the Blitz. Try as she would, she could not lose the idea that Edna had long ago lost some valuable music. She knew perfectly well that Edna, who had never heard of a gondola, had no more idea of such a romantic, soothing thing as music as she, Mew, had of being a big tough character like Edna. But the sense of Edna's loss persisted. She went over to the bleaches and said, 'Good afternoon.'

Edna bridled and turned away.

'You've not been about. Have you been ill again?'

'Again?'

'You said you were – well, often rather ill.'

'I'm always ill. I've been worse, that's all.'

'I'm sorry.'

'Upset.'

'Oh dear.'

'Depression. Very severe. And I've been chucked out.'

'Chucked out?'

'Of the bed-sit.'

'Oh – whatever for?'

'Staying out nights. Sleeping days. Lying about the parks.'

'Staying out –?'

'Yes. After that terrible business. I got upset. I couldn't go home.'

'Terrible business?'

'Yes. The accusation. When they took you up for the fish.'

'Oh Edna, they didn't. They didn't at all. They understood perfectly. I'd been – well, there'd been some sort of a hoax.'

'So, what sort of a hoax would that be?'

'Well – I don't like to –, I try not to think really. Whatever it was, I've forgotten it. But I told the truth and the official believed me. He was a very good man. A nice Scotsman. I expect they can tell, you know, if you just explain and tell the absolute truth.'

'You bloody, fancy fool,' shouted Edna at the top of her voice. She turned, thrust Mew aside, knocked down half a gondola of Sanilav and Mr Sheen and bottles and jars crashed to the floor. Toilet rolls bounced for miles. Purple in the face she lurched out of sight and the track of her across the huge store could be traced by the commotion.

Away she surged down the dog-meats, past the condiments and spices, through the toiletries, beyond the frozens and the household requisites and away towards the off-licence and the far check-out doors. There – quite out of sight now of Mew – there was the most unholy crash of falling Carlsbergs, a metallic, backyard avalanche of coke cans, and bells began to ring. People screamed and a man standing near Mew comparing the quality of different brands of baked bean, said lugubriously, 'It's a bomb.'

And when Mew reached the scene, there on the floor lay Edna, apparently dead, in a bed of broken glass like a great salmon on a bed of ice.

The crowd was drawn back from her, whispering and muttering, and into the silence while the odd can and bottle slowly rolled to rest stepped Mr Paterson and knelt by Edna and felt her wrist.

Mew knelt at the other side and, as Mr Paterson felt for beats, they both gazed at the fierce, unhappy face.

'She's dead,' said Mew. Mr Paterson said nothing. Then after a while he lifted a finger, 'Undo her clothes.'

'Oh!'

'Her macintosh. Her – whatever's underneath. Her – corset.'

'Is someone getting an ambulance?'

'Of course.'

'Is she alive?'

'Yes. It is a heart attack. 'I'm afraid – a – huh –'

'What?'

'She must have the kiss of life.'

And Mr Paterson bent his lips to Edna and it was quite awful.

Then, wiping his mouth with control, Mr Paterson began to burrow under the British Home Stores macintosh and massage Edna's heart and some Staff came along and put screens round Edna and Mr Paterson and Mew and outside the screens other Staff began to sweep up glass, because the off-licence and soft-drinks gondolas constitute a heavy-selling area of the store and even a quarter of an hour can cost.

'*Has* someone telephoned for an ambulance?' asked Mew again.

Mr Paterson was sweating and massaging away at Edna.

'Of course.'

'But are you sure?'

'Go and see.'

'Can I leave you?'

'Yes – go and see.'

Mew ran to the office where, yes of course an ambulance had been called. But it had to come from a distance and there was uncertainty among the ambulancemen about whether they were on strike, and the traffic was heavy.

'Ring again,' said Mew. They rang again and got quite an encouraging reply. Mew ran back to Mr Paterson – still massaging – his kind, blue eyes sticking out, staring over the screens at the sky above the Putney rooftops.

'Let someone take over.'

'No. No. This is my department. I am trained in First Aid.'

'But – you have been going for nearly half an hour.'

'She's still alive.'

'Who is she?' asked the manager. 'Is she your relation?'

'No. She's just someone –'

'We see a lot of her in the store. We've been having to keep an eye on her for some time now. You are sure that she is nothing to do with you?'

'Nothing.'

'I think she's going,' said the manager.

'No,' said Mr Paterson.

A siren was heard in the street and some men ran in with a stretcher and bundled Edna up. Mr Paterson fell back on his heels. He looked very worn.

'You go on off now, Paterson,' said the manager.

'No,' said Paterson.

'You next of kin?' the ambulancemen asked Mew.

'No, no. I was just – someone in the supermarket buying a few things. I'd like to know where she's being taken, though. What hospital.'

'Okay, then.'

The great load of Edna was carried away like a pharaoh to the Nile.

And rather like a pharaoh from the Nile within less than a fortnight Edna was installed – Mew did not quite know how – in Mew's dark little comfortable house in Werter Road, in Mew's front room in front of Mew's television set, beside Mew's double-barred electric fire, her feet up on Mew's great-grandmother's needlework stool.

Mew herself felt dazed – but there she was. And so very much better, her appetite excellent. She was even able, with help from Mew, to get up and down to the guest room, not used for years, with its pre-war eiderdowns and thick carpet scarcely stepped on since Mew's parents bought it before their wedding more than half a century ago. The stairs did not seem to tire her, but Mew thought it wise to take her her breakfast to bed every day for the time being, at half past eight, just an hour after she had taken her her early morning tea.

Edna's mind seemed to be equally unaffected and seemed scarcely aware of its brush with death. She scarcely referred to it. Mew herself felt shy of referring to it – trying only once to see if Edna remembered the valiant Mr Paterson.

'Such a wonderful man,' she said.

'Who?'

'Mr Paterson. He saved your life you know. Well, he gave you –,' (she looked away) 'the *kiss* of life.'

Edna continued unmoved to absorb Pebble Mill at One.

'It wasn't very nice for him,' said Mew, annoyed.

'Why not?' asked Edna.

'Well – he didn't know you. Doing an intimate thing like that.'

'People watching, were they?' asked Edna, stretching for biscuits.

'Well, some. Some didn't like to. It was upsetting.'

'Upsetting. *They* were upset?'

'Then,' said Mew, 'he began to massage your heart.'

'Massage my heart?' Edna's careful eyes veered round.

'For half an hour non-stop. Everyone told him to stop. That you were dead. He just went on. He was wonderful. A marvellous man. Aren't you going to get in touch with him, Edna?'

Edna turned back to the screen. 'They're trained for it. It's their job. After all, it was probably fumes.'

'*Fumes!*'

'Well, I was probably knocked over by fumes. They keep those supermarkets too cold you know. Can't spend half an hour in them sometimes, it's so cold. Fumes from the air-conditioning. I might be sueing them.'

'*Sueing* them!' Mew said. 'If you don't get in touch with that man then I will myself,' and she went straight out to make enquiries, coming back half an hour later unexpectedly despondent because she had been told that Mr Paterson had just retired. No, they couldn't say what his present address was – he had planned to take a long holiday. She could write in of course if she liked.

*

The next day she was surprised to find that Edna put on her macintosh and went out for a walk. After that she went for a long walk every day. First it was just for an hour, then a morning, then a whole day. At the end of the week she stayed out all night, and Mew also noticed that a pair of porcelain candlesticks was missing. The following week she couldn't find a little gold ring with a love-knot in it that had belonged to her great-aunt. Then – looking for her cheque book to write a cheque for the (very high) electricity bill, she found that gone, too.

She told Edna, who said nothing. She sought about desperately for someone else to tell. The police? That seemed extreme. The neighbours? She was not one for the neighbours. They were all so young and clever. In the end she went to the bank to stop the cheques, and the bank told her that it was too late, for all the cheques in the book had been used and three hundred and twenty pounds had been drawn for goods at various branches of Marks and Spencer.

'Three hundred and twenty pounds. But I must be over-drawn.'

'I'm afraid you are. We were just about to contact you.'

'But I never go to Marks and Spencer. I've hardly bought any new clothes for years.'

'I'm afraid these people do it,' said the bank manager. 'It's an old trick now. Usually it's picked up unless it's a really outstandingly respectable person. The thieves buy some garment with a false cheque. Then they return it a day or so later and say that it doesn't fit and are given the cash. This thief has been to twelve different branches. All over London and out of London. She's been as far as Slough. Have you any idea –?'

'Yes,' said Mew, 'yes I have.'

'You know that you can bring a prosecution?'

'I wouldn't know where to begin.'

'Isn't there someone to help you at home? Are you alone?'

'Quite alone,' said Mew and thanked him for his folder of information and instructions for legal procedure which she dropped hopelessly in the litter bin outside the bank. She knew that once home to the great monolith of Edna eating fish sandwiches over the fire, her skirt hitched to show the melon thighs above the good tan support-stockings, her eyes cool, knowing, watching Mew as she worked about – she knew that she, Mew, would do nothing. Something in Edna paralysed all action.

'I really do have nobody,' she found herself saying to the

newspaper stand at Putney East Station (and, oh God, she had said it aloud: like Edna at the bleaches), 'I have nobody,' and she bumped headlong and immediately into Mr Paterson.

'Oh,' she cried, 'Oh –,' clutching his sleeve, 'I've tried so hard to find you.'

He looked stern.

'To thank you. To thank you for –'

'For what?'

'Well, for saving the life of the woman. Of Edna.'

'Did the unfortunate creature survive?'

'Yes, oh yes,' and Mew began to cry and the story poured forth – the electricity bills, the fish sandwiches, the candlesticks, the ring, the cheque book, the bank manager.

Mr Paterson's square moustache looked frosty. 'You mean that she is living with you? This thief is living with you?'

'Yes.'

'She is there now? At your house?'

'Watching television. Yes – and eating. Well of course I must have asked her, but – you see the main thing is that I don't think she even likes me.'

'Having stolen your money –'

'She doesn't know I know it's her. Or maybe she does. It may be that she is – I have the feeling – testing me in some way.'

'Where do you live?'

'Down here – down Werter Road.'

'I'll come with you.'

Together they went down the High Street, past the supermarket and the Baptist Chapel which recommended on a noticeboard that God's grace was sufficient for them, and inside Mew's house found Edna at her ease. She turned her eyes on Mr Paterson but did not move.

'Out,' he said, 'out. I've heard all about you. Out. Where are your things?'

'I've nowhere to go,' said Edna, scratching the backs of her upper arms, knees apart to Nationwide.

'Can't be helped. Let's get your things together,' and he

was upstairs and downstairs very fast, carrying a battered suitcase. 'Is this all?'

'There's my Building Society Book.'

'I've got that. There's three hundred and twenty pounds in it. We'll be seeing about that, too.'

'There's stuff in the drawers, my provisions.'

'Stolen,' said Mr Paterson. 'We'll be seeing to them. Off. Out.'

Edna looked quite stately opening the garden gate but, turning, seemed to become very loose and slow, her clothes too big for her. She said, 'But where shall I go?'

'Nothing to us,' said Mr Paterson whose mouth had once been clamped on hers. 'You are nothing to us at all.'

'Mr Paterson,' said Mew, noticing the 'us' with a queer lift of the heart.

'Dixon,' said Mr Paterson. 'Name is Dixon Paterson.'

'I'm Muriel – Mew. Oh, but where *will* she go?'

They sat down side by side on the gingery velvet sofa in Mew's front room, the one on which she had wept, and stared long and hard at her brass bowl with the lemon geranium in it which stood on the revolving bookcase. 'Like those plants,' said Mr Paterson. 'Tricky though. Like a lot of sunlight.'

'I have no trouble with them. Oh, Mr Paterson, that poor woman. That poor woman Edna. She has no one. All lost in the war. All her records –'

'Records?'

'She doesn't even seem to know who or what she is.'

'She's a common thief, that's who she is and what she is is off her chump.'

But he looked thoughtful.

'Mr Pat – Dixon, I'm just going to look out of the gate.'

He joined her there and they saw Edna standing on the corner of Werter Road and Oxford Road reading a notice about an exhibition at the Putney School of Art. As they watched she turned away, stooping rather, and began to cross the road. In the middle of the road she stood still for a while before moving on. Then they saw her sit down on a nearby door-step. In the still-good macintosh, which Mew had had cleaned, and a turqoise toque, brand new, which had just recently appeared in her wardrobe, and decent leather gloves she sat there, serious and quiet, like someone in church. 'Oh Lord,' said Mr Paterson hopelessly (it was the moment at which Mew began to love him) and he set off down the road to bring her back.

*

She lived with them for nearly two years after they were married, causing considerable trouble and endless surveillance and some curiosity among their acquaintance – for after the wedding acquaintance did begin to collect. Mr Paterson was a rather popular, old-fashioned sort of man, good at Bridge. Mew found that she was rather good at Bridge, too, and there were some very nice evenings indeed in the front room watched over by the lemon geranium and Edna, huge and silent, only vaguely hostile, in her corner, reading bound copies of Mr Paterson's old wartime *Picture Posts*. Most people accepted her as some sort of dotty cousin.

And when she died – a resounding crash in the hall and too late for massage or kissing – both Mew and Dixon Paterson were taken quite unawares. The house – lighter, airier – seemed to be more ordinary, more empty. Somehow she had suited its side-street darkness and for some time after the funeral they crept about in it, bewildered and silent in a state of shock.

'After all,' said Mew, 'she brought us together.'

'Nut case. Off her chump.'

'But she did bring us together. And you know – in her way I think she did like us in the end. Stealing was just – well, what the psychiatrists say –'

'Psychiatrists,' said Dixon Paterson. 'She didn't give a damn.'

But, 'Poor old thing,' he said – they were going through Edna's things and he'd unearthed from a top cupboard a pack of forty dishcloths marked 'shelf 4a, Household'. 'And what's this? Looks like her will. Addressed to a solicitor.

Quite good writing. Good, educated writing. I think it's her records.'

They delivered it to the address stated and found that Edna had left them a very great sum of money and a large house let out to excellent tenants in Ealing – all properly signed and witnessed by two Philippino nurses at the hospital.

They moved then to an improved address, higher up the hill towards the Heath. Dixon bought a good car and Mew spent a lot of money on the garden which was much admired. The neighbours here were friendly and invited them to Sunday drinks, and although Mew found that she got their names mixed up, for they all looked so much alike, she was happy. Though she very much missed the easy shopping.

Ball Game

'D'you want to come to Auntie Pansy's?'

'Whoever's that?'

'My godmother.'

'What a name.'

'She had a funny father.'

'Very funny father.'

'She's funny too. A bit funny in the head. She lives in the suburbs. She's rich.'

'Has she got any heating?'

The college – Margaret and I were first term students, was cold in a London energy crisis. Every day there was a power cut. There was one blanket on each bed. On top of it I was putting my coat, macintosh and dressing gown. Margaret was putting coat, macintosh, dressing gown and hearth rug. London – the first time we'd either of us really been to it – was black with ice, dark skied, the trees firewood stuck in city stone. Not even the comfort of snow. We were both homesick.

'She said to come for the weekend and bring a friend. It's – well – there's absolutely nothing to do there, but we could take some work. The food's wonderful. She's got a cook.'

'A cook!'

'Yes. And a maid. They're both a hundred.'

'How old's Auntie Pansy?'

'She looks sixteen with grey hair. She's not developed. She's retarded. Oh yes – and we'll have to go to church. She's got a thing about vicars.'

'You know, I think maybe –'

'No. Do come.'

*

We changed trains at Earls Court and took the District to the terminus and then a bus into Surrey scrub. Margaret was in one of her fierce moods. She was disappointed in London University and so was I, but even with the weather, I wasn't disappointed in London. If I hadn't been so hungry (I hadn't a penny over my grant) or if I'd been able to afford some boots, I think I would have given up the weekend of ease so as not to miss London on a Saturday night – the Lyceum dance hall where I slunk off with a dreary boyfriend I'd known at school just to be there, or a theatre – any theatre, gallery or standing room, or a beer cellar I'd found off the Strand. Margaret didn't care for the idea of the beer cellar or the dance hall – she was a Scot. She was after truth, not decadence. I was after both and a few things more (I'm from Liverpool, and though we both knew that we hadn't much in common except our age, which was eighteen, we got on well. We had been put in rooms next door to each other on the same corridor. When Margaret was in one of her most homesick moods I could hear her thumping about and dropping things – I'd go in and we'd talk. She would give me a brisk nod as she went by on the stairs. Then we found that neither of us could bear the all-female screamings and twitterings and spinsterish gatherings over coffee and buns and the odd sinful gin and orange. We were both yearning for men of course, but it was going to be some time before we felt we knew each other well enough to say so. In fact we'd got some men by the time we talked about them. We were old-fashioned girls.

In the bus, turning from the vista of dead bramble bushes and sopping laurels, Margaret stirred at last out of gloom. She said, 'Oh, by the way – you know I said she was mad as a meat axe?'

'Auntie Pansy?'

'Yes. Well – she's not really. It's just over one thing. It's a sort of kink in the brain. She's crazy about her house. She thinks people are stealing out of it.'

'Is her house special?'

'No. It's utterly ordinary. Lush I suppose, but ordinary. Conventional – grand. It's just the same as the ones on either side of it – huge, Edwardian. Gravel paths and that. Fake mullions. Big square garden full of leathery stuff round the edges and an orange path and a terrible rose-bed dead centre. It's posh – in a posh road – a sort of hymn to imperial England. Very comfy. Her pa was a bank manager. She tries to keep things as they were.'

'Pretty difficult. Has she got television?'

'I think the maids have. There's a billiard room.'

'Lord!'

'With a big silk crinoline over the table. There are big silk crinolines over all the centre lights. The fireplaces are like cathedral doors and there's lots of standard lamps and a gong in the hall. And a row of pipes.'

'Pipes?'

'Her father's. He hated her. Her mother died when she was born so he hired a nurse and never spoke to her. She crept about the house thinking he was God. She didn't speak till she was about six – just giggled. The nurse had to go with her, even to the lavatory.'

'Heavens – till when?'

'Till she was seventeen.'

'What happened then?'

'The father died. Then the nurse died.'

'My heaven.'

'My father – he was the father's friend. Well, friend – my father'd been vicar out here, before he took to the kirk, and Pansy's father was his church-warden – he tried to get Pansy a companion. But she wouldn't.'

'Could she argue?'

'Yes. She just said no. "No, I'm all right. I've got Gertie and Betty. They can cook and shop and I can order the drink." '

'Drink?'

'Yes – it seems she'd taken to drink in a quiet way with the nurse.'

'Does she manage her money?'

'Yes. When she was twenty-one she wrote my father a letter – very school-girl-looking apparently but perfectly sensible – saying that she would take over now, and though she looks pretty funny, she gets along all right. Spends thousands on the house. Oh, and on the vicars and curates at the church. They do nicely. She's generous.'

I said, 'She sounds nice. Just because she's house-proud and likes vicars she's not mad. Probably no different from my mother. You don't know. They're passionate house-proud in Wallasey. Forever tearing off the wallpapers and sticking up new bits. Idiot beautification. Specific to the affluent West. Everywhere's not all Forties lincrusta and polish like Edinburgh.'

Margaret said, 'Well, just you wait.'

We crunched up the deep gravel to the big stained-glass front porch of MalvernLodge and the door swung back two inches on three chains to reveal the eye of what turned out to be a tall, whiskery woman in an antique cap and apron. A little behind her, round as and rather the same colour as a muffin, stood Auntie Pansy. She had a huge kind smile and untidy hair escaping from a shiny tortoise-shell hair-slide with a painted forget-me-not bow in it. She kissed Margaret and giggled nervously at me. Her hands clapped.

'This is Anne.'

'Yes.' Her head bobbed up and down.

'It's very nice of you to invite me.'

She giggled. The maid shut the door and we were enclosed in glorious warmth, our feet in the thickest, newest-looking carpet ever seen off the screen of a TV commercial. There was a coal fire burning in the hall fireplace and it flickered in the thick cream gloss of half a dozen beautifully painted doors.

'Oh – a fire.'

'Yes. And the central heating's not let us down. We had tons of coke – so lucky.' Huge cream-painted radiators beneath polished mahogany shelves were giving off blasts.

'There's a fire in the drawing room, too,' said Auntie Pansy, 'and crumpets.' I looked at Margaret to say without words, 'Mad – she's not mad. She's marvellous,' when Pansy put a little fat hand on my arm and said, 'Before you take your coat off you must come and see the new power point.'

'Oh – power point?'

'Yes.' She marched across the hall to a little round room with a sewing machine in it with a wrought-iron rocking treadle for the pointed shoes of long-dead sewing ladies. By the fireplace was an opulent electric fire with fake coals and by it in the wall a power point. 'We had to have it, dear. We had to have a new adapter. We think the old adapter got stolen.'

'It's lovely,' said Margaret, and we all paced out again.

At the foot of the stairs Pansy stopped. 'Would you like to see the pepper pot now or later?'

'What pepper pot, Auntie?'

'The one with silver bands. Your parents gave it to me on my seventeenth birthday. It's been mended. They'll want to hear about it.'

'Oh – later, Auntie.'

At the bend in the stairs she was still looking up at us. 'All right. After tea, dears. We are all so pleased about it.'

*

I said, 'Margaret!' flying in. Her room next to mine in a sort of guest wing was very like it: a huge bulging high bed with a rolled-over end, a bolster and several pillows. Six different sized towels on the rail, water carafe, box of biscuits with rick-rack tape stuck round it and *The Church Times* on the bedside table (I had *The Lady*). Margaret sat at a dressing-table with a dozen ivory brushes and combs (mine were silver) and her mantelpiece was covered as mine was with framed photographs. 'It's heaven. It's perfect. It's History. Look at the tassels on the curtains. We haven't the right clothes.'

'Oh – don't mind.'

'The bathroom – have you seen the bathroom?'

'Of course I've seen the bathroom. I've seen it every year since I was born. We have to come here for a week every summer.'

'The *shower*! Four inch thick glass. All black and silver. Pure Alma Tadema. It's like in a museum. It's hardly been used. *I'll* never dare use it.'

'No. I shouldn't. Or be careful anyway.'

'The taps! Silver lilies. And the black tiles on the ceiling.'

'Wait till you see the loo.'

'Well, I'll have to use that. In fact now. Where is it?'

'Ours is next to the bathroom. Hurry up. There's the crumpets. Look, change your shoes.'

'When I've been to the loo. I'll join you downstairs.' And I flew out.

But I had not changed my shoes when I joined them in the drawing room. I had completely forgotten about shoes. It was nearly ten minutes later and in the hall mirror I saw my face ashen.

'There now,' said Auntie Pansy. 'We've started, but there are lots of crumpets. Lots of crumpets.' She waddled to the black and gold bell handle in the wall and began to push it about like a gear lever. 'More crumpets, please,' she said to whiskery Gertie.

('Wherever've you been?'

'Oh,' I said, 'God!'

'What?'

'I can't tell you. I can't tell you.')

'Are you enjoying college?' asked Auntie Pansy, waddling back to her arm chair and Margaret had to tell her all whilst never taking her eyes from my face. When Pansy turned away again, once to ring for hot water, once to look for her knitting, I mouthed in torment and Margaret's eyebrows went up and she mouthed furiously back. When Pansy was summoned to the telephone which was kept in a special domain, I exploded with a moan, nearly tipping the tea table over, 'Oh my – Oh, Margaret! Oh!'

'What on earth –?'

'Margaret. Oh God – Margaret!'

'Are you ill?'

'I wish I was. Or dead. Oh Margaret – I've smashed the lavatory.'

'*Smashed!*'

'Smashed. Yes. And blocked. Blocked it.'

'How?'

'The ball. The ball.'
'My God,' said Margaret. 'Not the ball.'

*

I had done this. I had entered the WC and subsided on its wondrous rosewood seat, the size of an ox's halter, gazing at the looking-glass walls on every side and even on the ceiling, the rose-pink sheepskin carpet at my feet. It was an unnerving sight – myself enthroned to infinity on four sides and up above. I wondered how Auntie Pansy got on in here after her drinking with the nurse. It wouldn't be the place to visit after a party. I arose to pull the silver linked chain which had a large, black, solid, rubber ball hooked on to the end by a silver hook. The ball had a glossy, *fin-de-siècle* sheen, lacquered to look as if it were wet. I didn't feel I should touch it and pulled the chain itself – a long heavy one, dangling from the black tank above and the ball sprang off the chain and disappeared down the lavatory pan.

Just like that.

One minute it shone like an astrolabe among the million mirrors, as it had hung for half a century. Then it was gone. The waters settled. The ball was there no more.

'I've got to tell her. I've got to tell her now,' I said. 'If you don't do these things at once, you never can. It's the only way.'

'No. Wait. We can't. She might go wonky. Let me think.'

'Oh Margaret – I'm sorry.'

'It's not your fault. It just happened.'

'Why to me?'

'Probably nobody's used it for ages. It's the guest loo. You gave too big a pull. It's not a house for vigour.'

Auntie Pansy came back and said we might like to change for dinner. We did – and sat at the shiny table in silence and the dinner was beautiful but we hardly knew it. 'Look at the pepper pot, dears,' said Pansy. 'I wouldn't have liked to lose it. The girls and I can't take changes.'

She ate hugely and we had two bottles of wine. She said little, but now and then, when she caught our eyes she gave a friendly, silly sort of laugh. When the silences lengthened, however, she was able to break in quite expertly with some sort of remark and it didn't seem to me – even through my haze of guilt – that Pansy was as dim as she made out. I began to think she knew already about the disaster, and was waiting.

We all had coffee round the fire and went to bed early. Upstairs Margaret and I went solemnly together to view the WC. We looked at all the multiplicity of shining ball-less chains in all the mirrors. We didn't look at each other.

'D'you *know* it's blocked up?'

'Well, it must be. It was huge. And heavy.'

'The drains'll be huge, too. They were massive in those days. Try pulling.'

'Never. Never.' I bent my head against the glass wall and closed a million pairs of eyes. Margaret pulled the chain which functioned excellently. Then Margaret began to make the noise of a dying animal and fled to her room. I followed to mine, put my head under my bolster and moaned. Gertie and Betty passed by on their way to bed, and we heard them say it was nice to have some young folk around and some laughing.

A mahogany and silver breakfast, a ride to church in the rain in a hired car that called each Sunday, a sermon about renouncing earthly things by a parson with red lips. Outside the church's cold white windows the rain soaked down into the suburban streets in such minute drops it seemed to seep rather than fall on the earth. The porch was cold. The red-lipped priest had soft, unused hands. 'Don't be late,' Auntie Pansy said to him, with a little skip. 'He's coming to lunch,' she said in the car, 'with his friend. In half an hour.'

'I shall die,' I said as we waited. 'Look – can't we get it done with? Let me tell her. Oh God – can't we replace it? She'll never go in there. She's got one of her own. Can't we send one for Gertie to put in without her knowing?'

'No – they'll notice it tomorrow morning, when they do the rooms. It's all they ever do – the rooms. And cook.'

'They'll think I stole it – or you stole it. You'll never be asked again. She'll not leave you her millions.'

A flurry downstairs told the arrival of the Vicar and his friend and we went down. 'The Vicar, ha, ha,' said Pansy. 'You've met. And this is Father Gary.'

'Hullo again,' said the Vicar without looking at us. He had his head in the drinks cupboard. 'Now then, Pansy, what do these girls like? We know your tipple – Bristol cream.'

We said sherry please, and I could see Margaret's stern Scots eyebrows draw down at the way he called her Pansy and old enough to be his mother. He gave us both sherry – very expert at knowing where the right glasses were – and poured himself a large one. For Father Gary he poured a generous Scotch.

'Water today, Gary?'

Father Gary smiled and said, 'No, no.' He was a small, short-legged man with the face of a film star. He wore his cassock and a big ring and had admirable eyelashes.

'A good congregation,' said Pansy deftly, shyly.

'Yes, yes,' said the Vicar, dismissive, leaning back. 'Now then Pansy, what about Italy, eh?'

'We're going to Italy,' he said in our direction. 'Pansy's taking us to Italy. Kind aunt you've got.'

'Godmother. Yes, very.'

'The three of us are going,' said Pansy, blushing and Father Gary gave a sparkling smile.

'Venice, Florence, Rome, Assisi,' said the Vicar.

'What about the house?' asked Margaret, and Pansy's smile trembled.

'Oh, one of my team's coming in,' said the Vicar. 'One of Gary's lot, eh? To keep the girls company.'

'Do they know – Gertie and Betty?'

Auntie Pansy looked insecure on this point and took out her hairslide and played with it. 'Not quite settled,' she said. The Vicar re-filled his own and Father Gary's glass.

He did a lot more of this during the lunch, which was enormous and delicious and so old-fashioned that there was stuffing in the chicken and syrup sauce on the pudding. The clergy did it proud, Father Gary excusing himself and leaving the room for a moment before the cheese. 'Excuse me a moment' and 'Thank you' were the only things he did say throughout his visit. Oh yes – and 'Black, please' over the coffee.

'Must keep awake for Evensong,' said the Vicar. They left – the vicar also disappearing for a minute whilst Gertie was fetching their warm dried coats – at four-fifteen.

'Time for tea,' said Pansy brightly. 'Now, what did you think of Father Gary? He's breaking all the girls' hearts.' She giggled as if she were repeating what everyone was saying but what was nonetheless excitingly naughty.

'I thought he was awful,' said Margaret, and I wanted to hug Pansy as her face crumpled. She looked lost and scared.

'He's – they're making a fool of you, Auntie. Look – I'm just going to get my books. I want to do an hour's work before we set off back.'

'So should you,' she added to me, but I was glaring at her and shepherding her godmother back to the drawing room.

'I'll join you,' said Margaret and went off. She stayed away a long time. Pansy and I ate anchovy toast.

'That's all right then,' she said when she came back. She sat down opposite Pansy and helped herself with self-confidence to a huge piece of cake, then gave me a satisfied glare and a sharp Scotch nod.

Pansy giggled.

'Didn't *you* like Father Gary, Anne?' she said. 'And the Vicar?'

'Oh –'

'They're very highly thought of. They're very good at visiting. The vicar rather reminds me of your father, Margaret.'

Margaret exploded in her cup of tea.

'No – but so kind. To take me to Italy.'

'But you're *paying*, Auntie.'

'Yes – but they don't mind. They say they'll show me everywhere. They know all the best hotels. They say we'll never drink water except for brushing our teeth. I've not been abroad since Nannie –' She touched her hair and the tortoise-shell forget-me-nots began to descend.

'Well, I've not been to Italy,' said Margaret. 'Anne's not

been to Italy. Lots of people – I'm sorry but I just don't like them, and I don't trust them.'

'Shut up,' I said. 'Margaret –,' and Gertie came into the room.

'Can I have a word please, Miss Pansy.'

'Oh – yes, Gertie.'

'*Private*.'

'Oh –' She pattered out and almost at once there was a great henhouse outburst along the hall.

'I've fixed it. It's okay,' said Margaret. 'Say nothing.'

'What on earth –'

'The ball. I've fixed it.'

'Heavens, I'd almost forgotten –'

'Well, I suddenly remembered. There's another. A ball just like it in the gents. Downstairs. I went in just now and prised it off. It took some doing. It was on tight. But it was on a hook and I got it off. The one upstairs must have been loose. I went up with this one and hung it on our chain upstairs.'

'But now there's one missing in – Oh my goodness!'

'In the gents. Ha!'

Auntie Pansy stood in the doorway.

'Is something wrong, auntie?'

Her eyes were wild.

'Yes. Oh dear. Yes, dear, I'm afraid – something very bad, dear.'

'Heavens, what?'

'I'm afraid –' (Gertie stood behind with a severe mouth and there was a flurrying suggestion of Betty behind again), 'I'm afraid that the ball in the gents is missing.'

'Ball?'

'The ball on the chain. Like the one you have upstairs, dears. It's irreplaceable.'

'Gone – it can't be gone.'

'Gone. If it had been yours I could have understood. That one is rather loose. It might even have gone down the bowl – it was solid enough. But this one – It was very firmly fixed. For *men* to pull.'

'When they remember,' said Gertie grimly.

'Whoever would want to steal a ball from a lavatory chain, Auntie?'

'Oh, they might. They very well might. It was an original Crapper from the King's Road, Chelsea. Father was very pleased with it. About 1924.'

'I am afraid,' she said, turning away with surprising resolution, 'that we have had a thief with us this afternoon.'

*

Margaret said that we must go and pack up our things and we climbed the stairs, solemn as aldermen, as Pansy stood awash in the hall. She looked up at us and said, 'Italy,' and walked sadly away.

I was subdued in my bedroom. I felt that Margaret was, in hers. I sat on the bed and looked at all the photographs of Victorian and Edwardian people. There was a great pompous one – father; a wispy, droopy one – mother; a terrible moony one with wet eyes, dressed as a nurse – Nannie, presumably; and several small-eyed, tight-lipped men in officers' uniform and several clergymen. I thought of Pansy's dreadful life. I wondered if she'd think of taking Margaret and me to Italy and we could give her a really lovely time. Then I realised that no time we could give her would bear any resemblance to the excitements of the Vicar and Father Gary and that between us we had deprived Pansy of the nearest experience she would ever have to romance. I thought, we shall be punished.

And then I heard the shriek.

Margaret came tearing in from the direction of our WC. 'Oh Christmas,' she said. 'Oh Anne! I've been to our loo.'

'Well?' said I.

'I did it, too,' said she.

A Seaside Garden

I thought of Helen Gibb the other day. It was on York station. There was simply nothing on York station to remind me of her. It must have been the tone of a voice passing, or maybe the airy, breezy smell of the North again.

There she was before my eyes, so living, so alert, so clever – oh, and such thin stick legs, such big boat shoes! No ready-made shoes could ever have fitted those fingery feet. Fourteen she was and I was fifteen. I'm forty now.

She arrived several days late for school her first term, which is a bad start and makes you stand slightly apart for a time. She was put in the desk next to mine, and I looked at her sidelong. She was so thin you feared for her – tall and gaunt with huge, spidery, round glasses too loose for her fine long nose. Slowly, slowly they slid down the nose to the very end of it and she pushed them back with a bony red finger. About every five minutes. During French.

Her face was red, too – two round red blobs on her cheeks, high up on her cheekbones. Her lips were bluish. From behind the wiry palisade of the glasses her eyes looked at you, round and bright sky-blue.

The French teacher's little finger lacked a nail and she always chose that finger to point to the places on the page where you were making mistakes as she walked around the class. Some girls shivered and some girls laughed and some girls retched. I used to close my eyes and think of other things. But when the finger landed on the book of Helen Gibb she turned her long, quizzical face in my direction and the glasses flashed. 'Hoo, hoo, hoo,' she went. A hooting laugh.

It was not popular. Not popular at all. 'Why are you laughing, Helen Gibb? You will write these out again. Twenty-five times.'

'Hoo, hoo, hoo.'

Her courage and amusement at the defective finger amazed us.

*

It was a school set at some distance from most of our homes in a small, gone-to-seed little town along the coast, chosen probably because it was central to the majority of the country neighbourhood. Almost all of us came in by bus and train, and in our class Helen Gibb was the only one who lived in the town itself. In the evenings and at the weekends she had no friends among us. This, and the fact of her late arrival tended to make her seem more different still.

At the end of every day, when we were gathering together to go for trains and buses – it was the rule that we walked in little clusters – Helen would slide past us and set off walking towards one of the forbidden parts of the town – smiling and moving with a queer, weaving sort of walk – to her house somewhere, we gathered, along the promenade. She was odd and solitary, but not unfriendly, though she didn't join in with anything much and she was excused all games.

She was tremendously clever. Smoothly the long red fingers turned the pages of her book. She would look up sometimes, gazing at nothing, reflecting, staring out of the window at the sea-birds and the sailing sea. Her writing flowed out neat and confident and faultless and when we were still starting question one, page one, of end-of-term exams, she was already asking for more paper. The little finger landed only that once upon her French book and at the end of term she got about 100 per cent in every subject. And six months younger than the rest of us.

'Hoo, hoo, hoo,' went Helen Gibb, unselfconscious and thoroughly amused. We thought that next term she would be moved up higher and we'd see an end of her – but no. There she still was.

This time she had arrived early and had been put in the front row near the only effective radiator. It was the cold spring term, the influenza and bronchitis term of this bitter cold, East-wind town, and she wore thick wool stockings and two jerseys over our come-day-go-day school uniform; but her body still looked all sticks and bones. Her cheeks burned with the bright red spots and her lips were lilac. At break times she was excused going out and sometimes so – with any luck – was I, not because I was ever ill but because I could simulate any disease at any time if there were a chance of staying in and reading a book.

One day I was hanging my arms down the back of a radiator, balancing a Henry James on top of it and sneezing professionally at intervals when there came through the gloom towards me, Helen Gibb. She picked along in an elderly-looking shawl affair – salmon pink over her gym-slip – a flamingo in wrappers. 'Hoo,' she cried, 'Henry James! The old silly.'

'I love him.'

'How much have you read?'

I said, '*Portrait of a Lady* and *Turn of the Screw*.'

She had read all Henry James. All Kafka. All Joyce. All everyone.

'James was not male,' she said. 'Not male enough.'

'What?'

'Henry James.'

At fifteen I was still awash. 'Not male?'

The light from the nearby glass door of the art room shone on Helen Gibb. It seemed almost to shine through her as through some amoebic water creature, thin and glassy as a Blake. She seemed all spirit.

'Not male enough?'

'I'd want more blood and sinew in a man,' she said.

'But he's a – great writer. A genius.'

'Hoo, hoo, hoo.' She began coughing.

She was not at school for most of that spring term – just a day here and a day there. I can't imagine now why we never talked about it. Every morning the form teacher called the register and hardly ever was there an answer to Helen Gibb.

'Anyone heard how Helen is?' she asked once, after two weeks. Nobody had.

So Easter came and the summer term – the short term. A hot, still, wonderful summer that year. The playing fields had grown a great crop of hay and this was stacked all around the outside of the field in little hay-cocks. Over to one side the crust of the tennis courts had burst up here and there in little pink volcanoes (it was an easy-going sort of a school) with daisies and dandelions sprouting out of them. All the school windows were flung wide and wafts of piano music or a teacher's calling voice at a blackboard went floating over the sea. Soon, as the heat grew surprising, we began to have classes out of doors, little groups in circles of chairs on verandahs or in the corners of the quadrangle. Bees buzzed, a lazy page flapped. Beyond the hay-cocks at the end of the cricket-field a slow train lolloped by. The sea whispered and shrieks came from the fives-court and the hurdles, where girls leapt and squeaked and flung themselves about in white shorts and bright green aertex shirts. In spite of the hot sun and all the indiarubber feet the grass grew thick with cowslips and white milkmaids. A wondrous summer.

Helen Gibb and I sat watching it one day. It must have been the Trials for the school sports which I had been excused on account of a twisted ankle worthy of the Royal Academy of Dramatic Art. We leaned against adjacent hay-cocks reading our books, with the summer sounds in the distance. Helen looked different. She was still thin but no longer skeletal, her cheeks less brilliant, her lips less blue. She seemed to mock less, observe more kindly. She sat thoughtfully, a book always open on her knee. Looking back, I know that I was perfectly aware that she was separate from the rest of us in some way, but it never consciously occurred to me, and certainly I never said anything about it to the others. We none of us, in spite of her curious appearance, her dotty face, her hooting laugh ever discussed the matter. In this animal disregard for sickness we were children still.

'What you going to do in the holidays, Helen?'

She pushed up her glasses. 'Finish Scott,' she said.

'No. I mean, where are you going to go?'

'Staying here.'

'Aren't you going away?'

'We can't. Because of the shop.'

'Oh.'

I hadn't known there was a shop. I had never conjectured. If anyone had asked me I would have guessed that Helen lived in one of the lovely houses backing on to Liddell's Woods – the houses with the fake Tudor gables and the bottle-glass windows and the great sweeping gardens and the tradesmen's entrances. They were my dream houses at that time.

'I don't mind,' she said. 'There's the sea. And the Public Library.'

'Do your parents – never go away?'

Helen put *Guy Mannering* face down on the hay and lay back with her eyes shut. Her sand-shoes had a quarter of an inch of space all round their tops and her legs stuck out like stilts. Her jaw-bone stuck up in the air and her spectacle lenses were table-tops. She looked fearfully weird and I wondered again why we never laughed at her. The skin on her stretched, long neck was so fine that you could see the network of blue veins. If she drank wine, I thought, you would see it going down. Like Mary Queen of Scots.

'Do your parents keep the shop?'

I was nervous. I was asking directly.

She said, 'D'you want to come round?'

'Come round?'

'Yes. To tea or something.'

'Oh – yes. I'd love to.'

'On a Saturday or Sunday?'

'Oh, yes.'

'It shall be done,' she said pompously, then, opening her eyes she watched me for a minute before beginning to laugh. She laughed as usual, the silly hooting cry, and I wondered for a moment if perhaps there were something in it that we hadn't liked to recognise – something desperate or frightened. 'Hoo, hoo,' she went, and again it became a fit of coughing, but so bad this time that she struggled to sit upright and then I had to hurry over to her and slap her back. I felt the bones down her spine and the back of her rib cage, and hitting her seemed horrendous, destructive, like beating at a fragile basket chair.

Gasping for air, she said, 'Okay. Leave it. I'm fine.'

'You don't sound fine. You sound like Keats.'

'Oh him. It wasn't so bad for him . Little short back. He'd have been in a spot with a lanky old framework like this.' Her glasses had fallen off and she lay back in the hay exhausted. She said, still gulping, 'How *could* Fanny Brawne?'

'How could she what? Helen, are you okay?'

'How could she not? Do it with him. Mean bitch.'

She sometimes said things like this, and it always shocked me because the the coarser she tried to be the lighter and more musical her funny clear voice. 'Do what with him?'

She opened an eye and grinned.

'Hey,' I said, 'Helen, d'you know who you look like now? Virginia Woolf.' Without glasses the line of her cheek-bone curved up very fine and pure. Her hair had come loose.

'Virginia Woolf! No thanks. There's another of them.'

'Another what?'

'Scaredy cat. Not doing it. Just because she was going batty.'

'We don't know –' (I wriggled. I was hopeless in this sort of conversation.) – 'We don't know exactly that she didn't do it. Only that she didn't have any children.'

Helen slapped *Guy Mannering* over her face to keep off the sun. 'Well, maybe she did,' she said. 'Maybe she had a child. What about that?' I saw the eye looking out from under the book. 'Maybe she had a little teeny baby while she was reading Greek in a turret. Lytton Strachey was its Pa and it had long thin feet and a long thin beard.'

'What happened to it?' I wriggled more.

'She took it down to the river and she hid it in a little basket woven with rue and ladysmocks and things that shepherds give a grosser name and Lytton said, "Oh by the way Virginia, whatever happened to –?" and *she* said, "I decided to give it to that common little Carrington. . . ."

' Helen –'

'Well, I can't do with these flimsy women.'

'Would you have done it, Helen?'

'Not with Lytton Strachey I wouldn't.'

'No – I mean, say, with Keats?'

Looking at her lying there, ethereal, weightless in the hay, her monastic fingers clasped on her utterly flat chest, it seemed an astounding idea.

'Oh Lord yes.'

'And with Leonard Woolf?' I who worshipped Virginia Woolf had always thought how beautiful and saintly it was, the Woolf chastity.

'I'll say. I can't stand V. Woolf. I don't know how she couldn't, with that lovely man. So sexy and smashing and Jewish. And then –'

I suddenly realised how odd this conversation was – these thoughts from the spare frame, the superb brain. They ought to have been – well, more intellectual, less like the rest of us. Yet she was being more explicit than Mabel Greaves who went with soldiers on the sandbanks.

'Do you want to marry someone like that, Helen? Like Leonard Woolf?'

'Oh no,' she said, 'he was heaven. But not my type. My type's the kind that knocks you about a bit.'

Silence from me.

'It was terrible, Virginia Woolf,' I said because I was now very bewildered and embarrassed, 'for them both. All that madness. And then the suicide.'

'It was a great sin,' said Helen, 'getting rid of your life like that.'

'We can't judge.'

'Oh yes we can. She didn't fight them. She let them get at her. Close her in. With so-called love.'

'Let who get at her?'

'The fates. The furies. The big, fat fates.'

*

I was to go to tea with Helen on Sunday afternoon, early, about two o'clock. She was to meet me at the station.

'Or if I can't my father will. One of my parents. Probably Pa.'

'How will I know him?'

'He's fat. He'll be trotting about. Steam rising. If it's mother she's fat, too. And she's got red hair.'

'You don't sound much like them.'

'No. I'm adopted. I'll be there myself though. It's just in case.'

And she was at the station standing by the barrier in a pink cotton dress hanging straight, like a stick of rock, and an antique floppy hat. I too was in a dress I had never worn at school, in honour of the occasion.

It was queer, nevertheless, being in the town on a Sunday, for it was hard to believe the place existed without all of us whirling about in it, and I showed my rail pass to the ticket man quite guiltily. I felt rather shy with Helen, too, glad when we took a different direction from the station from the week-day rat-run and walked down an out-of-bounds road to the sea. Then we walked along the high promenade, then down and into the no-man's-land under the railway bridge. Then beyond the town along the cliff top and into a bending, climbing road of white, lavatory-brick houses – a sort of white back-street. They were poor houses, narrow and mean, but their line and curve and all their faces lifted to the sunny day were rather beautiful. So were their narrow strip gardens, each with a little stick fence and wooden gate. The gardens – twelve or fourteen I suppose – were all different, some with scarlet beans on tents of sticks, some just hard mud patches with rusty tipped-over tricycles, one with a sagging washing line and a rabbit hutch. Next to this one was the most superb garden, bursting and bulging with colour and life, springing out over its fences, showering out on every side, roses and honeysuckle and buddleia and big, branching acacias.

'Ours,' said Helen, opening the gate.

All up the path there were leathery hydrangeas, violent blue, heavy pink, lavender and white. Along the other side was a flat border of outsize velvety pansies, chocolate and yellow, like appliqué embroidery. On the tiny, migraine-green lawn in the middle stood a vermilion plaster gnome, several giant plaster toadstools, a rustic bird-table and a short, stout man with his back to us. He was on his haunches, piercing a narrow strip of soil with a wooden spike at regular intervals. Beside him was a watering-can and a heap of frail, weed-like things about to be planted. 'My father,' said Helen Gibb.

He spun round, knocking over the can, looked first at her, anxiously, rather wildly, then at me, and began to pump my hand up and down and talk at top speed.

'Well I never! Great thing this. Friends, eh? This *is* a day. Must find Mother. All right, dear, then?'

'Fine,' said Helen.

'Not tired? Well now. Hydrangeas. Like hydrangeas?' He was looking me up and down with critical attention.

'They're wonderful. I've never –'

'Don't see them round here much. Don't grow on chalk. Special feeding. Special soil. Peat. Chemicals for colour. Have to work at them. My word yes. Not tired?'

'Oh – oh no.'

'Mother. Where's Mother?'

A large, slow woman came out of the house and stood looking at us. The two big, stout people in the tiny garden with the backdrop of the meagre house were like a child's first painting, out of scale, as the flamboyant growths and scents seemed in turn to be too heavy for the little garden. Beneath the forced plants one felt the exhausted, ransacked earth, the stimulants and artifices poured in to bear the great burden of richness. 'Ovaltine?' said Helen's mother, 'I've got Ovaltine.'

'Oh – thank you – but –'

'And some malted biscuits. Just to set you on till tea.'

At home we had had roast beef and Yorkshire pudding and a treacle sponge an hour ago.

'Actually I –'

Relentlessly, the large slow woman turned to lead us into the tiny front room. Mr Gibb followed and after a noise of the washing of hands in the kitchen came and sat with us round a low table. Mrs Gibb came pacing, smiling, with two steaming cups of Ovaltine. She twitched the curtains to let in more sun. The sweet, bedtime, sickroom smell of Ovaltine filled the room. The windows were tight shut. The carpet in the cardboardy room was red, the sofa and chairs were gold sateen and the cushions, stuffed to bursting, were green and gold brocade. There were gilded things on the walls, a huge dangling centre light of brass and false candles. Helen watched as I lifted the huge cup of hot drink to my mouth, her bright eyes laughing.

'Helen, you're to have a drink now before you go up.'

'Go up?' said Helen.

'You said you'd both be looking at the books in your bedroom. Then you'd have a little sit on the prom.'

Both parents turned big faces to her. Pleading faces. I saw that they both looked old – too old to have a daughter of Helen's age. Or perhaps they had grown old.

'No. We're going to walk through Liddell's Woods and home over the sandbanks.'

Both old people looked down at their hands. Mr Gibb unclasped his for a moment and then clasped them again. The room grew still. I knew that no quarrels took place. They had all run themselves out long ago, being impossible. It was a house, I saw, in which all passion had become inexpressible, being dangerous for Helen. She had the two parents in the palms of her deft hands, in the tips of her long fingers. But in the cocoon of that sitting room, lean and alien as a giraffe, she watched them nervously, once again taut. You cannot stop me or there will be a storm and I can't have a storm. Yet if you don't stop me I'll go miles over the sandbanks and may never come back. I will be ill again. You will be watching, waiting, fussing, agonising, not knowing for hour after hour. So leave me be.

She was being cruel to them with a studied, expert cruelty, perfected over years. Gentle Helen Gibb.

'I don't want to go all that way,' I said. 'The sandbanks are miles. I'd rather go up and look at the books.'

Helen raised her eyebrows. Then she began to hoot. To

laugh in her crazy way, her light eyes bright, her cheeks brighter, and at once both father and mother looked up. The mother said, 'Oh, if Helen wants to go –,' and the father, 'Now then. Now then, Helen. Go if you want. Go if you care to. You know how it is –'

'It's just there's a nice tea,' said Mrs Gibb, 'I shouldn't want you to be late. I've a nice salad tea planned for five o'clock.'

All three now looked at me for the decision, and I felt lost. I said nothing. At last Helen got up lazily and went over to the window.

'Can't we have some air in here?' She fiddled with the catch through the net curtains.

'There's a cold wind,' said the mother. Helen lifted the curtain on to the blinding flowers and the airless day. She yawned.

'What do you really want to do?' she asked over her shoulder.

(Get away. Out of this house.)

I said, 'Well, if we could look at the books after tea, could we do *half* the walk? Just maybe go as far as the houses by Gillson's Woods?'

'Okay,' she said, and loped out of the house and down the path to the front gate which she leaned on, saying no goodbyes.

The father and mother accompanied me down the path after her, one on each side. We walked crowded up between the hydrangeas and the pansies. 'Careful – to be so careful,' the father said. 'Well you'll understand, of course.'

'I don't really.'

'Well, you'll have seen,' said the mother, a soft plump hand on my arm. 'A marvel. A little miracle is Helen.'

'It's Mother's the miracle. Mother's the miracle,' said Mr Gibb. 'But for Mother Helen would have never left the cradle. Oh but Mother's worked. How she's worked.'

'We've all worked,' said Mrs Gibb with slow content-ment, 'we've never given up. They said she'd never go to school you know.' The plump hand's pressure became heavier, and I stopped. Mrs Gibb fixed her eyes on me and said with terrible pleasure and resolution, 'Now they say – she has about a year.'

I thought we were very much within earshot of the gate. Helen, without raising her voice, said, 'If we're going, shall we go?' flung it open and loped off ahead of me, so fast I had to run to catch her.

'Hey – wait.'

She was walking with her arms folded, her chin on her chest, her great long feet pad-padding, one-two down the terrace, her glasses watching them. But she couldn't hold the pace for long and by the time we'd reached the high path that led to the woods she was walking as she did at school, the queer, painful, weaving walk, feet almost crossing over each other. Now she was wheezing.

'So you see,' she said, 'the completed picture.'

I said no.

'Well, you knew there was something?'

'I don't know what I know.'

'Well, you must be daft then. Would you put up with it? Being treated like this? A set-up like this?'

'But what is it? The illness? Is it a secret?'

'Oh the *illness*. I don't bother with the illness. It's nothing. Wonky heart. They love it. It keeps them going, my wonky heart. It's their purpose in life. It's the illness they love, not me. No, I mean how would you like to be messed by people like them?'

We meandered slowly past the splendid houses, set back behind the wrought-iron gates – great smooth lawns, stone terraces, huge urns and large, polished motor cars sleeping beneath cedar trees. 'You do know I'm adopted?' said Helen.

'Yes. You said. But they're obviously very fond of you.'

'Oh my God yes. Well, they're fond of something.'

She stood looking through the grand gates of a more than usually over-dressed 1920s house. 'All day,' she said. 'All night. If I get out of bed for a glass of water they're there in the door.'

'How – *exactly* ill are you?'

'In my view I'm not exactly ill at all. It's just they're

nurses. A couple of born nurses. They had nothing to nurse so they got me. They're sick. Sicker than I am.'

We turned back along the quiet road and she was breathing hard and her face had flushed into patches again. I saw, behind the queer, mild-looking face and the glasses that her eyes were furiously angry. 'They won't win,' she said.

We went away from the woods and down towards the sea for a long way, and I saw that we were going along the edge of the sandbanks. 'We're going a long way round, aren't we?'

She said, 'Not really. We're not going *over* the sandbanks.'

Soon we came to the bulging-out cliff and a zig-zag flight of wooden steps, old railway sleepers stuck here and there in twos and threes, scattered lackadaisically up the slope. I hadn't expected this last bit. These were secret places of the town to me, and I was a bit lost. At the top of the steps, I thought, there must still be a fair way to go.

'What time is it?'

'My watch has stopped. I'm going to sit still awhile.'

'They'll be worrying. Oughtn't – do you feel all right?'

She stared out to sea. She didn't look all right. Her purple mouth was drawn up tight and her eyes were shut. I could hear her breathing. I felt frightened. 'It's remote control,' she said. 'They're here. All the time.'

'I think you're mad,' I said.

Then, 'Shall I get someone? Go on up?'

'No, it's all right.'

We sat side by side. Her hands gripped her bony knees. I noticed her watch and saw that the second hand was going round. The watch said half past five.

'Helen! It's half past five! Your mother –'

'Okay,' she said, 'go on then. Go ahead and I'll follow.'

'Can you? Up all the steps?'

'Yes, I'm fine.'

I began hurrying up the cliff in little runs, this way, that way, up the dizzy track, looking back once or twice. After a time I saw that Helen was standing up, then slowly starting after me.

At the top I saw that I was on the part of the promenade that tipped down under the railway bridge and I ran fast, under it and on, and at last reached the white brick terrace. In the road outside the exploding garden two men stood and Mrs Gibb stood just inside the gate. I ran as fast as I could towards them calling out at the top of my voice that Helen was just coming. While I was still a long way off I saw Mrs Gibb stretch out her hands and then slide down inside the gate. Mr Gibb turned to her and then back to me. The second man, a neighbour, put the little dish he was carrying down in the road and ran to Mrs Gibb as I called, 'Look, it's all right. She's just coming on slowly. We're just late.'

Mr Gibb opened out his arms in a helpless way, turning like a queer, plump clown towards his wife, then back towards me, and as I got nearer I could see he was in a tremble of excitement and had tears in his eyes like a baby.

'She's all right? She really is all right?' I felt he was going to embrace me.

'Over here,' said the neighbour. 'Over here now, Ernest. See to her. She's in a right faint.'

He hurried over and the two of them made a poor attempt at lifting her up, 'Fainting eh? Oh dear, oh dear. Whatever next? Oh Lord,' said Mr Gibb.

I went over, too, and then I turned away. I was very used to fainting women in novels, but this was the first one I had seen, and it was not pleasant. Mrs Gibb looked flaccid and dead. A slow clacking noise came out of her mouth, and some dribble. She opened silly eyes.

'Fainting?' said Helen coming up – it seemed to me she was there quite fast. Her cheeks were bright and she was breathing hard but she looked lively, even excited. Happy, if anything. She stood in the little dish in the road and broke it in two. One half said RAB, the other half BIT. 'I've broken the rabbit dish,' she said. 'Hoo, hoo, hoo!'

The neighbour, a man in braces with a black haze of stubble on his chin, said, 'You could be more careful, Helen.

You're right bad to your mother. Sending your friend running all alone.'

'Oh – it's my fault,' I said, 'I'm sorry – I never thought. Shouting out –'

All four of them looked at me unblinking and there was a silence of agreement. Then Mrs Gibb, heaved up now and holding tight to the back of the gate, stretched out one hand and felt the air like a blind person and began to cry. They steadied her, the men, and shuffled her up the path, Mr Gibb taking care to avoid the needlework pansies.

I said to Helen, 'You knew. You made me go running ahead by myself on purpose.'

'Of course I didn't.'

'You did. You were creating a scene. Look – it's late. I'm going home.'

'I'll come to the station.'

'No. Tell your mother I'm sorry. About missing the tea. You'd better go and rest or something. Take some pills.'

'I never take pills.' She seemed glowing with health.

At the end of the road I looked back and saw her thin, tall figure standing by the broken dish watching me. In the train I found that I was nearly home before I realised I had started. I opened our front door and walked in to our empty sitting room, picked up Henry James and lay on my back with my feet propped half way up the mantelpiece, glorying in the silence.

'I don't care if I never see her again,' I said to the page. 'I don't care if I never see her again,' not imagining that it would be true.

*

On the Monday her desk was empty, and she was absent all week. And the next week. And the next. I wondered about her, and as the term passed I found that I was thinking about her and her parents and the vibrating house by the sea rather a lot. My mind began to drift to them in class, in the train going home, at home, in bed. One evening I thought of the telephone and got up in the middle of a History essay and looked in the phone book. But the Gibbs were not on the telephone.

Then I wrote a very, very late thank-you note to Mrs Gibb, saying that I was sorry I had had to leave early and I hoped she was better. I did not ask after Helen. I received no reply. In the end I wrote to Helen. Again, no reply. Just before we broke up I bumped into the French mistress in a corridor. She steadied me with the hand with the missing nail which had pleased – or frightened – Helen so much.

'A little more care, child. A little more care.'

'Please,' I said, 'could you tell me what has happened to Helen?'

She looked very serious and her painted mouth pursed into a rose. 'Not very well,' she said, '*not* very well.'

That is all I heard. It is all I heard for years, for before the next term great events had occurred in my life and driven all else from it. My father's work went South and within weeks, after all my fifteen years, we had bought a flat in unknown Notting Hill, sold our house, left our friends and the world had contracted into London. And only now, a quarter of a century on, standing on York station, I suddenly thought of Helen Gibb.

And I thought – I'll go. Why not? It's not far. I was on the way to Whitby on Library business and there was to be a car for me to borrow. I would go tomorrow. No – I would go this evening after dinner – drive back along the coast road to the school, see the old promenade and the terrace of sharp white houses once again.

It was high summer as it had been the last time – a lovely, light, Northern evening – and I drove along, astonished at myself for being so moved by it all: the hideous red and black school house, now an old folks' home – the same old back yard door where we'd gathered for the train, the promenade, the sea, the sweep of pale, featureless coast. Along under the railway bridge I drove and the white terrace was there, dazzlingly familiar as a recurring dream, bending away, leaning back from me up the slope. It was smarter than twenty-five years ago and the gardens had grown very much alike – little postage stamp lawns, little squares of clipped privet, or beech-hedge or even box. The doors were painted architects' colours and there was a spiky riff-raff of television aerials along the roofs. There was no clue as to which had been the abundant Gibb garden until I saw a solitary, out-of-step garden with dipping clothes line and rabbit hutch which must have been the one next door.

As I looked at this unashamed garden the door of its house opened and a lean old man with braces and a white haze of stubble on his chin came out and bent to the rabbit hutch with a bowl. Then he shambled down the path and leaned on the gate. He stood staring out at the sideways sea as if waiting. His mouth chewed.

I got out of the car and I said, 'Excuse me. We've met before. A long, long time ago. You've hardly changed.'

He said he didn't remember and I said he wouldn't. 'But I know you're the same man,' I said, 'I'd swear it. I'd swear you've been here twenty-five years.'

He said, 'Seventy.'

'And you knew the Gibbs. Next door. A – kind – couple with an adopted daughter.'

He said, 'She weren't adopted. I remember the day she were born. She once smashed my rabbit dish.'

'Oh, I knew the Gibbs,' he said, 'I knew them all right.'

I said, 'Could you tell me – what happened?'

He scratched his ear for a while and continued to look past me at the sea. 'Well, of course she died,' he said.

'When was that?'

'Oh, years back. Years back.'

I said, 'Poor things. Poor Mr Gibb.'

'Aye,' he said. 'But he was soon over it. Sold up the shop and went off. Went off with another woman, matter of fact, six months later. All over her he was. A poor-looking thing. Lost track of him.'

I said, 'But poor Mrs Gibb. Whatever did she do?'

'I tell't you. Mrs Gibb died.'

'*Mrs Gibb* died! Was that before or after?'

'Before or after what?'

'Helen dying?'

'Oh, Helen didn't die. That Helen didn't die. She's done well. Married rich. She's got half a dozen kids. She lives in one of them houses backing on to Gillson's Woods.'

The Pursuit of Miss Bell

'Miss Bell is having an awful time. Between ourselves,' said Fay Stout to her friend Mrs Walker.

'Miss Bell?'

'Oh awful. Between ourselves.'

'Is she worse?'

'No – not worse. She's being bothered by a man.'

'By a *man*? Miss Bell?'

'Yes. It's not very nice I'm afraid. He comes to the house. Knocks on the door. Then he just sits in the garden.'

'She hasn't got a garden.'

'Well, on that wall. The wall across the front step. Sits with his head twisted, looking at the sea.'

'Head twisted?'

'Yes. You know the streets all run down away from the sea. I don't suppose Miss Bell's seen the sea for years, poor soul.'

'Well she's diabetic.'

'Yes. Not that diabetics – but well, you know how she is. She's agrarian or whatever its called.

'Whatever's this man? How d'you know?'

'The maid told someone. I'd rather not say who.'

'Father Clark.'

'Well, there now. *I* never said it. Isn't it dreadful? And they're supposed to be trained you know. In the theological colleges. Not to talk. They have classes on it. Secrets of the –'

'That's the Romans. D'you mean Father Clark told you –?'

'Well, he thought I might help. Help Miss Bell. He said he needed my help too.'

Fay Stout lifted her solid body up from the haunches with pride before letting it subside again. The two women were taking morning coffee in the Public Library. They had chosen their books – two each, and one for Miss Bell.

'I'm going round to Miss Bell with the library books,' she said. 'Now, as a matter of fact. Ought I to say anything d'you think? Lead up to it? I mean if it's anything.'

'You'd think Father Clark would have got in the police.'

'I think he'd have liked to. But – well, it's not very nice.'

'What?'

'Well, Miss Bell. You see, she's not objecting. She's not minding him, this man sitting on the wall. The maid says.'

'Maybe she's not noticed him.'

'Oh yes she has. The maid says. She gets up and walks over and looks at him from behind the blinds. And at night she stands in her bedroom by her dressing table, looking down.'

'At *night*!'

'Yes. It seems he's still there at night sometimes. He just sits.'

Mrs Walker slowly picked up her coffee spoon and stirred her coffee.

'Perhaps he's after the maid.'

'Don't be ridiculous,' said Fay. 'Old Charlotte.'

'Well, old Miss Bell for that matter. I mean really. She's a bladder of lard. She must be sixty.'

Then both together they said, 'Very rich of course. Very rich.'

They looked into each other's eyes.

'Has Father Clark said anything to her?'

'Yes – he's tried to bring the conversation round.'

'He's clever if he can *have* any conversation.'

'Oh yes, but you know he's been visiting her for years. I think he's always done most of the talking but –'

'He always does.'

'She just sits. You know how she does, poor thing.'

'Well, I've always had a very soft spot for Miss Bell,' said Mrs Walker firmly. 'She's very kind. And she has those beautiful water-colours.'

'She has some lovely furniture, too. I wouldn't know about kind.'

'Well, she's got a very kind face. Kind expression. She always gives a pound to Christian Aid. They say she's a millionaire.'

'What – in Partridge Street?'

'Well, she won't know it. Her father left her nicely.'

Mrs Walker went round to Partridge Street and it was a cold day with sand blowing off the beach and snaking down the empty road and its pavements and getting in one's eyes. The houses were white brick with heavily net-curtained windows, most divided into flats and displaying cards saying 'Vacancies'. Only Miss Bell's house had a single shining doorknocker and knob. It had immensely old, slatted Venetian blinds kept very clean. On the gate, hardly six feet from the front door was a lozenge-shaped notice saying 'no hawkers, travellers or circulars' in black enamel. The low wall alongside the terrace gate had once had chunky black iron railings, but these had been sawn off in the War to make machine guns or saucepans and only their roots remained. Beside one of these bumps of old iron a man sat. He got up and walked away as Mrs Walker approached. With a flip of a long coat he was round the corner.

Mrs Walker regarded the maid sternly as the door opened and the maid looked sternly back.

'There was a man on the wall.'

'He'll be back,' said the maid. 'He's been here off and on for weeks.'

'Don't you tell him to move off?'

'It's not my directions.'

'This,' said Mrs Walker, 'must stop,' and she proceeded to the front room where Miss Bell sat in a green, mossy-looking, wood and velvet chair, waiting for her lunch which the maid was cooking in the kitchen and which smelled delicious.

'There was a man sitting on your wall,' said Mrs Walker and no nonsense. 'Here's your library book, Miss Bell. Charlotte says he's often here. You ought to get the police.'

'Hello, Mrs Walker.'

'He had a very funny look. Queer long coat. He'll be from one of those Cheshire Homes. They've opened a new one.'

'Is that my book?'

'Yes, it is. It's another nurse and doctor. Miss Bell, we're none of us safe these days you know. Even you who don't go out. I've just been having burglar locks put on all my windows. Wherever you go you hear of break-ins. There was a time when none of us would even lock our front doors when we were in the house. Now there's not a house in The Drive without an alarm. Box on the wall. Unheard of in father's day.'

'I never liked The Drive,' said Miss Bell unexpectedly.

'I hope you have locks on these windows.' And Mrs Walker went across to look through the slats of the dustless blinds and saw the man sitting on the wall again. He had short, sandy hair and large ears. He sat hunched up.

'I shall go out now,' said Mrs Walker, 'and send him off. It's too bad, Miss Bell. You shouldn't be pestered like this. Too bad – helpless as you are.'

'I'm not helpless,' said Miss Bell, 'not altogether. He's just – somebody sitting.'

'But it looks so dreadful.'

'Dreadful?'

'Well – a man. Hanging about. Like a – dog. Look. Look at him.'

But although Miss Bell was quite capable of walking, though slowly, she made no move from her chair. She watched Mrs Walker instead with her round almost colourless eyes – an utterly passive woman all her life, perhaps because of her sickness, perhaps, thought Mrs Walker, because she is really quite simple in the head. She was a woman everybody pitied and accepted and did what they could for – in the excellent way of the Anglican church. Calling. Chatting. Making a life for a woman with no family and the difficulty of great possessions, taking her to church each week and one or other helping her fat, unused body up to the altar rail. Sometimes they even fought for the privilege. Mrs Walker would say to Fay Stout, 'It's my week for

Miss Bell,' and Fay Stout would say, 'No dear, it's mine.'
They would take Miss Bell out to buy new clothes, too – to
very expensive shops where she was pampered into silk or
crêpe – once into a fur stole which she had never been seen
to wear. Afterwards they took her to a good hotel where she
paid for a substantial tea for the three of them and sherry
afterwards. They never asked more, though Mrs Walker
had told everyone openly that she had asked for the painting
of the Chinese shipwreck in Partridge Street because her
grandfather had been coxswain of the lifeboat on that
occasion. Miss Bell served a purpose in the place, apart from
her interesting wealth, in providing a source for disciplined
charity to be stored away for self-congratulation when life
looked bare.

'I'll send him off,' said Mrs Walker again, and Charlotte
and she went out on to the front step.

But the man again was gone and Mrs Walker turning to
tell Miss Bell the fact, saw that she was smiling.

*

The Vicar called on Fay Stout the next evening, muffled up
against the spring. He propped the bicycle against the wall
of the house, carefully padlocked it and rang the chimes. He
accepted whisky and sat frowning. 'There's rather bad
news,' he said. 'I don't like to have to say this, but something
rather out of the common has happened in Partridge Street.'

'Miss Bell again?'

'Yes.'

'Mrs Walker is afraid she's not safe.'

'Did Mrs Walker get in? When was this?'

'Get in? No – she just called. Yesterday with the library
books again.'

'Was Charlotte there?'

'Yes. Cooking stew with green peppers.'

'Fay – Charlotte's not there now. She's left.'

'Charlotte! After twenty years!'

'Yes. She came round to me. She said it was all beyond her
now and she couldn't cope. I left her at the vicarage and

went to Partridge Street but I couldn't get in. Miss Bell was in. I could see the television screen glaring. I could hear it. But nobody answered the bell.'

'She's slow on her feet.'

'Yes. But she wasn't alone. There was – this man. The man was there. I saw him in the house.'

'Through the blinds?'

'Well, not through the blinds. The blinds had been drawn up askew at one side and you could see directly into the room.'

'Did he see you looking?'

'Well, it was not quite like that. I looked in and saw Miss Bell. Then I felt someone looking at me. As one does. From – well, from upstairs. He was looking down. He did not answer the door. He would not answer the door and when I shouted out he just moved away.'

'It's – Vicar – it's terrible! What – could you *see* Miss Bell?'

'I banged on the window. Yes. Yes – I could see Miss Bell. She was – in her green chair, just as usual. But she had her shoes off and her feet up on a stool and her skirt – rather awry. And –'

'Oh!'

'Yes. She was eating sardines out of a tin.'

'Whatever do we do? Inform the authorities?'

'I'm afraid I have tried. They say Miss Bell is quite out of their jurisdiction. She is not certifiable. She has invited the man into her house and he cannot be charged with loitering with intent. She cannot legally be considered to be in danger.'

'But she is. She must be.'

'She might well be, I agree.'

'Who is this man? Is he from the Cheshire Home? Is he – well, he might be a pervert of some sort – a murderer. I saw a film –'

'He's not from the Cheshire Home. We've made enquiries – in Partridge Street and all round about. Nobody knows him. Someone – the fish and chip shop – thinks he has a bed-sitting-room along the promenade. He eats fish and chips every night and then goes and sits on Miss Bell's wall. He's perfectly well-behaved.'

'However did he – I mean – choose her?'

'Charlotte says that it was that sunny day in March. She put Miss Bell out on the step in a deck chair with a book while she was turning out the sitting room. When she came to get her in for lunch, the man was sitting on the wall.'

'Were they talking?'

'No – no. It appears they were just looking at each other.'

'I expect he was looking past her into the hall. There's that lovely clock. And the Chinese Shipwreck.'

'Very likely.'

'I'll speak again to the police,' said the Vicar, 'but I know what they'll say. There is simply nothing – I have also been to the CAB – that we can do.'

'But she's alone with him. In the house. He's upstairs. In the – in the upstairs. And Charlotte's gone.'

'Charlotte is in a considerable state of shock. I'm sending her to her sister in South Shields. She said she just – I'm afraid this is very delicate, Fay – she just went in to see to Miss Bell the other night, to get her her whisky –'

'Whisky – I thought she was diabetic?'

'Well, no. I don't really know how that got about. It must be very slight. She's lately been having a whisky last thing. Well, the man was there. She had let him in. She was out of the green chair and side by side with him on the sofa. They had a tumbler of neat whisky each and the bottle between them on the floor. They were watching Newsnight.'

'All I can hope,' he said as he unfastened the bicycle padlock, 'is that Sunday may bring a change. I shall call each day of course, but if I can't get in let us pray that she will be ready for you on Sunday at ten-thirty.'

'It's Mrs Walker's week for Miss Bell,' said Fay Stout, 'but perhaps we should both go.'

In bed that night, however, she thought, 'I'm damned if I'll do anything,' and between sleeping and waking, the hazy picture of Miss Bell in unspeakable delights troubled her dreams.

'In that bedroom,' she thought, 'with her mother's portrait, and the crucifix!'

*

But the church saw nothing of Miss Bell that Sunday, Fay Stout or no Fay Stout, because when Mrs Walker called alone Miss Bell was sitting on her back doorstep shelling peas and not answering the front door. When Mrs Walker came round and rattled the back yard door and called, looking through the little grille set in the wood, she continued to shell, saying nothing, not looking up. Mrs Walker had already tried the telephone which must have been off the hook, for it was continually engaged.

Miss Bell seemed very calm. She looked over once at the frenzied latch of the back door, jerking up and down. Then she looked at the man who was standing over by Charlotte's compost heap down the end of the yard, kicking the compost about. Three high, white brick walls surrounded the back yard. The man's face was very white, too, with an almost luminous look, his hair so short and bristly that it was almost invisible except when the sun caught it. His skin was as pale as Miss Bell's, though Miss Bell's today looked a little different. There was a cast of colour over it. She sat straighter on the step. Around her were dirty milk bottles. A heap of washing-up stood and could be seen just inside the kitchen window. Past her, down the hall, Mrs Walker could make out newspapers and letters dropped through the letterbox on to the mat, unopened and unread.

'It's me. Madge Walker, Miss Bell,' she cried from the back street and watched while Miss Bell finished podding the last pea and then, looking down at the peas, began eating them one by one, delicately from the basin. The man, in time, came and sat by her on the step at her feet, rubbing pale hands in his almost transparent hair. She handed peas and he took them by ones and twos, and sometimes she presented a little handful, and they ate them between them until they were finished.

'It's not right to deprive yourself of Church and friends,' cried Mrs Walker through the grille and the man went into

138

the kitchen and came back carrying two cans of beer. He passed one down to Miss Bell and she took it from him with a nod and smile.

*

'I've remembered who he is.'

'Good God, Fay, it's the middle of the night.'

'Vicar – I've remembered who he is. I knew I'd seen him. It was before your time. In Father Barker's time. It was that man who kept on going to prison. That misery.'

'What man? Wait. Light on. Wire tangled. Wait a minute.'

'Before your time. There used to be a man who was always turning up in church. To sleep. We used to find him in a pew late at night or early in the morning when we unlocked it. The only place he had to sleep. Good suit – quite a – gentleman.'

'Fay –'

'In and out of prison he'd been. For years. We always let him have a wash in the church hall. Someone usually gave him some money. He was – oh dear, – he did smell.'

'Ha! What had he done? What did he go to prison for?'

'We don't know how it started. But when he came out he couldn't find work and he used to hang about trying to get back to prison again. They told us once – I remember – he went to Woolworth's and stole a clock and just stood. Stood there in the doorway – by the glass doors – till someone came to arrest him again. Hopeless.'

'Old lag.'

'Yes.'

'Ha. Well, we'll think – think again in the morning.'

Fay Stout thought on then, however, for hours, remembering more of the man with his white, soft hands and how she had found a towel for him and made him tea once or twice in the Hall. He had never spoken to her, or looked in her direction.

*

By Easter time it had come to such a pretty pass in Partridge Street that nobody called for Miss Bell for the Good Friday service. 'Well, there is no point,' everyone said. On Easter morning Mrs Walker was filled with a rash and powerful feeling that she would do nothing, plan nothing about the Eucharist, the great obligatory celebration. On the rather dismal afternoon of Easter Day – the blankest moment of Holy Week – it had almost been a ritual to gather with one or two other ladies, Miss Bell among them, but Fay Stout went instead to spend the rest of the day with a cousin some miles off and Mrs Walker went with her dog along the beach. The Vicar rested.

All three separately noted the bleakness and cold of Easter Day and wondered why it was usually thus and Good Friday so beautiful. 'It is too white a light, too much to bear,' thought Mrs Walker on the icy beach, watching the steps taken by her excellent shoes, the sheen on the coat of her dog. She thought of her wonderful health, safe bank balance, faultless reputation, her life, useful and sane. Calling the dog, watching the sea come in, so depressingly eternal, she thought, 'Resurrection – oh God for something now.'

It was on Easter Monday morning that someone came to the vicarage – a landlady from across Partridge Street – to say that someone had better come.

'The door's wide open,' the woman said, 'and the back door's open, too. You can see right through to the yard. There'll be folks in stealing. Maybe have been.'

'When did you notice?'

'Yesterday. In the afternoon. We thought they must be round the back. But there was no lights on last night. The door's stood open till morning. We're opposite.'

'The house is a shambles,' said the Vicar after a quick look around the ground floor. He came out to report. The two friends of Miss Bell and Charlotte (who had returned to work at the vicarage) stood muffled up and grim. The gate with the enamel lozenge defying hawkers, travellers and circulars swung and creaked in the wind. 'There's no one to be seen,' he said. 'Come in and we'll go upstairs.'

Upstairs grey sheets, soft with no washing, slid from the bed. Clothes were tipped everywhere. In the bath more dark clothes soaked with a stagnant smell. There was nobody there, though the presence of people was still powerfully about, and in the bedroom the portrait of Miss Bell's mother was propped against the wardrobe. The crucifix was in its place. One of Miss Bell's big, ginger support stockings was draped over a reading lamp. 'This is more than I can bear,' said Mrs Walker. She looked in the lavatory where the body of the man hung from the chain, neatly, like old, dried tobacco leaves. It was a poor, undersized body. Fay Stout, coming up, was astounded by her terrible satisfaction.

The shoes were touchingly blocky, boyish-looking, the kind given prisoners on release. They hung like weights. 'I remember the shoes,' thought Fay Stout as Mrs Walker felt for the stairs and Charlotte began to scream.

*

Miss Bell was found far away down the beach towards the old breakwaters where the Chinese Shipwreck had taken place, and was walking here and there apparently untroubled by her agrophobia, for she could be seen from far away with the wind and the white sand blowing all around her. Seagulls swooped crooked over her and the black piles of seaweed were crisp as burned noodles. On the far sand hills the bent grasses clattered and Miss Bell's thin bits of hair strained away from the sea likewise, as did her clothes. She wore no coat or shoes and only one stocking, but she had her glasses, and, as she walked and paused and considered, she bent now and then to examine small things upon the beach – a pebble, a stick, a shell, a little twist of driftwood, an empty coke tin.

She was very cold when they reached her and smiled at them when they took her to the hospital from which she never came out. She moved – after tests – to the geriatric ward. She answered no questions about the man, or anything else, and she showed no emotion when she was asked about her house and what she wished done with it. 'Nothing has been touched,' they said. Nor had it – not the clocks or her mother's jewellery, the silver, the turkey rugs or the enormous quantity of expensive unworn clothes. Fay Stout acquired – nobody thought the worse of her – the fur stole and Mrs Walker was given – quietly – the Chinese Shipwreck.

They continued to visit her, and the Vicar three times a year brought her the Sacrament, which she ignored. Once or twice, when the sun shone in the hospital gardens, which the geriatrics did not often sit in because old people need heat, the nurses said that Miss Bell would smile. Sometimes, too, she wept, but they jollied her along and she soon stopped. Nobody disliked Miss Bell. She wasn't a bit of trouble to anyone.

The Last Adam

Venetia strengthened herself at the airport by repeating prayers which she was disturbed to find all came from the Order for the Burial of the Dead.

Trying for words of thankfulness, all that came were words of conclusion. 'Then cometh the end,' she repeated, 'when we shall have delivered up the kingdom to God.' She tried to heave Mother Clare's battered suitcase, which contained everything that Mother Clare possessed, on to the airport scales: but Mother Clare's old jaw set tight as she put Venetia's manicured hand aside and gave a heave herself, tutting with regret that she could do no better. A strong, man's hand, with raised sinews along the back of it came down over the nun's hand, and laughing whitely a boy lifted the case on two fingers. Lean Sister Agnes stood palely by with her own belongings – a box and a bag at her feet and a none too clean paperback (*Lord of the Flies*) clasped in her hand with the passport and ticket. Sister Ambrosine, scruffy and weeping, stood already at the checking-in desk, her chin just reaching the counter, her glasses steaming with tears in the heat of the coming monsoon.

The three old nuns were being recalled from the sub-continent to Oxford. Their Anglican order – branch-line and cranky – had been founded more than forty years ago. Its base in Drab was to be merged with a rather larger and more effective one in Calcutta. As India was accepting no more missionaries the three nuns, quite of an age for retirement, were going home to England and Venetia Craig, the lay co-ordinator of the order had flown out from Oxford to see them off, tie the last knots and turn the key in the mission hut. Her report would be written back at home after a stopover in Calcutta.

The great age of the three women did not show so much in their faces as the sense of the smallness of their bodies under the full, traditional nuns' habits they still wore, long after almost every other order had abandoned them. It gave them a look of having been superseded – particularly by the Catholic, Mother Theresa nuns who flitted everywhere in Drab, in the filthy streets and about the Catholic precinct with its flower-beds and stone lace screens and palms. These are top nuns, thought Venetia. They carried about with them an air of success the Oxford nuns had no inkling of. The Oxford nuns had chosen to work across the railway line at a hospice called the Hospice of the Last Adam – Venetia had not seen it yet – very hard to find in a mess of alleys and shacks, little publicised.

It was not – Venetia had been told – very well-run nor had been for some time, for Sister Agnes, designated house-keeper when she first came out to Drab in 1938, had not been good at keeping accounts. When Venetia had asked her about accounts during the past two days at the hostel in the centre of the city where the nuns had been spending their last few days and making their farewells, she had only looked vague. 'I was a bad choice as housekeeper,' she said. 'At home in Shropshire in 1938 my family had a house-keeper you know – and a cook and housemaid. I had always hoped to work with Indian babies. I suppose of course it has been good for me. And someone had to do the housekeep-ing.' She did not add that she had become a harder, tighter-lipped Sister Agnes when she had realised that her dull job had not been for her soul's benefit but because Mother Clare was too spiritually advanced for accounting and Sister Ambrosine would have been worse than hopeless.

So – through the Second World War which scarcely touched the Sisterhood of the Last Adam, and through two internal Revolutions in the country, when there had been gunfire round the Intercontinental Hotel and dive-bombing over the river as the other Europeans tried to get away, the three women had continued to live in their tin shack nursing and teaching a little, once trying to start up a small factory for the making of nails. Reports continued to be sent home more or less annually, and when the cross on the Hospice door fell off Sister Ambrosine painted another and Sister Agnes nailed it up again. 'We create a presence,' Mother Clare had said, 'a Christian presence.'

And this was true. Their village had accepted them at once, grew used to them and though what they were there for was rather unclear sometimes, it was in a landscape where the importance of systematic, recordable events was always in doubt. The nuns were absorbed as natural phenomena. They grew skinny and brown as the people about them and lately, as founder patrons in Oxford died off and contributions fell, as underfed and cold in the evenings.

'They are even cold now,' thought Venetia, mopping her neck with a handkerchief. Despite the steam on Sister Ambrosine's glasses they had been three cold hands that she had shaken as the old women passed through the grubby cardboard door to the astonishments of the X-ray machines and the customs officials patting bodies for drugs and weapons.

Venetia hoped that the nuns would not be patted.

She turned to see the two suit-cases, the bag and the box totter off uncertainly on the conveyor belt through another hole in the cardboard screen, turned back to watch the last rusty flutter of Mother Clare's habit, the child's face of Sister Ambrosine lifted unhappily, her hand waving in the wrong direction. Sister Agnes, holding fast to *Lord of the Flies* was striding away. 'We brought nothing into this world and it is certain we can carry nothing out,' said Venetia unoriginally to God.

The crowds closed in around her. A large political group, some in dark suits and watch chains, some in dhotis, jostled around the cardboard doorway, chanting something patriotic and waving flags. Beside her, two old men suddenly knelt upon the ground and sank their foreheads against the floor. Near them another man undid the top of his pyjama trousers and held them away from his body for air, his mouth moving in devotion. Above his head a paper notice pointed to a Prayer Room and Venetia could see it, packed to its doors with people praying for the travellers. They, the politicians, the crowd generally – even the hundreds of faces pressed against the glass outside the airport behind Venetia's back – the legless and armless beggars, the pimps and the touts and the rascals and the porters – all looked at home in a way the stateless nuns did not, that she did not. The nuns, she thought, had not even looked as if they were going home. 'Hear my prayer oh Lord,' she prayed, pushing up the blue and green bangles on her folded arms, gripping each elbow with her bright pink nails (the nuns had been charmed with her: 'How *pretty* lay missionaries are now,' they had said), 'Oh Lord, with thine ears consider my calling: hold not thy peace at my tears. For I am a stranger with thee, and a sojourner as all my fathers were.'

She took a rickshaw back to the hotel – it was the rickshaw of the boy who had helped with the suitcase – and then sat in it for a moment, thinking before getting out. It was only eleven o'clock in the morning. She might do well to go now and do the final inspection of the Hospice. She needed no lunch. She would probably find little to be done. The shack, Mother Clare had said, was quite empty, and all that was necessary was that she should have seen that the door was locked – and perhaps just make certain there was no sign anywhere of Sister Agnes's accounts. Then she would come back to the Intercontinental to rest her jet-lag (it was the third day, the day when it bites) beside the swimming pool.

She gave the bicycle rickshaw wallah the address and asked him to drive her there.

His dazzling smile, she thought, will mean that he's never heard of it and she said, 'Very well. I will get other rickshaw wallah.' After all, it was going to be a long way. He probably only knew the beat from the airport to the Intercon, which was exhausting enough. She took out a wad of dollars.

But the boy smiled on and nodded, twisting himself up again on the saddle and the tricycle flew off again, down the Commercial Road.

Venetia leaned against the coloured butterfly plastic of the rickshaw and looked at the boy's curls and the points of his shoulder blades through his white cotton shirt. His bony hands were beautiful. Now and then he would turn his head and smile at her and the white scarf attached to his shirt floated over his shoulders. He had a bold moustache and merry eyes. 'He's like Young Lochinvar,' thought Venetia, and looking about her saw Young Lochinvars everywhere as the rickshaw traffic thickened in the environs of the Old City. Looking at her on all sides, from all levels – from high windows in the desolate palaces, from the street stalls, from the dark caves of the mud floored shops were beautiful young men, openly wondering and admiring.

'Admiring,' she thought, 'what nonsense. I am forty-two. Older than any of them. The expectation of life here is thirty-four. And I must look a grotesque – long and thin and gaunt and pale. I wasn't a model in Rome for nothing. To them I'm a giraffe.'

All around her were other rickshaws jammed with saris, sometimes four or five together, mothers and children squashed in tight like dolls in a box, layer upon layer of rose and flame and hard turquoise nylon and net and silk, only black eyes and nose-rings showing, even the feet covered. 'I can hardly look female,' she thought. 'They probably have to think twice to see I'm not a man.'

She took out lipstick and, as they flew away across the main highroad that intersected the Old City, grazing a bus, nearly tangling with a herd of black goats threaded on to a string by a naked baby who padded along with them down the mainstream highway, she painted her mouth – observed with distaste by a great bronze moth of a woman in the rickshaw alongside.

Towards the railway the traffic thinned a little and as they approached the line her driver slowed, put his bare feet down on the earth and stopped.

'Okay?' he said.

People were very busy on the railway line, sitting on it, praying on it, engaged in earnest conversation. One old gentleman was carefully re-tying the enormous turban of another. On the level crossing the crowds were thick and some people had put up a table over the line itself and were eating a meal. On either side, straggling away, were children selling fruit from upturned boxes. The rickshaw boy disappeared, leaving her on the crossing with the crowds gathering round her, looking, edging nearer, gentle but determined, like cattle homing in on a picnic.

Six or seven children climbed nearer her, then on to the tricycle, up behind and on each side of the seat. They clung, touching her feet and hands. One got hold of her wrist with the jade bangle and her watch. They talked fast, fighting for space, like starlings and she tried to show her lack of fright by talking smilingly back in English which they didn't know. Only when she felt the watch strap being loosened did she sit up straight and shout at them and at the same moment the boy came back. Shouting and aiming unrealistic kicks at the children he deposited in her lap apples and bananas.

'For my wife.'

She thought insanely that it was a proposal. Then she laughed, 'Your wife – you are too young.'

'I take you to my wife. To both my wives. And my baby. Of one week.'

'But we are going to the – to where the Sisters lived. The Last Adam.'

'Yes. Lasadam.'

'You *know* it? I thought you'd never – ?'

'I brought in the nuns to the Church hostel two days ago. Then today to airport. They know me. Teach me English. I their friend. I live here.'

'I'm lucky,' said Venetia.

They smiled at one another. Talking all the time over his shoulder, he pedalled on and she lay back again hearing only occasional words on the wind – Ambrosine, Motherclare, Jesuschrist. The heat of midday grew and she felt the sweat under her thighs, running down her arms, between her shoulders under her linen suit which stuck to the coloured plastic. 'I hope the colour doesn't run,' she thought, 'I wish I'd brought a hat,' and she put on dark glasses and pulled the crackly concertina top of the rick-shaw as far as it would go, trying to shade her bleached hair – hair dried out by long ago sun in Africa, like grass, the badge of all her ramshackle travels.

'It's my first time here,' she called.

'First time Drab?' He laughed over his shoulder. 'Drab no good. You take me home with you? Take my brother. He work in your house. Nobody want Drab.'

'Drab's no worse than Calcutta.'

'Ha – Calcutta!' he yelled back as if he had said, 'Ha, the moon and stars.'

'Look,' she said, 'Drab will grow better. There's the new airport.'

They were passing great diggers, piles of stones, the rubbish and clutter and cranes and JCBs gathered like an army on the new runway. There was a great pile of stones to be turned by hand into gravel, but nobody was working.

'Too hot to work,' called Venetia.

'Not too hot,' called the boy. 'Work stop for murder. Big trouble. Just re-beginning.'

The rickshaw turned away from the construction works at right-angles, on one wheel, along by a wire fence and on to a broad piece of waste ground with no path across it. An old man, naked, picked rags out of a heap of rags. Several women, squatting apart, beat coloured rags with stones beside a dark green pond. Men chattered amiably together in a row, defecating into a trench, and swarms of children seemed to rise out of the mud and scummy water to watch Venetia pass.

The children began to jog and run along beside the rickshaw, looking up at her and calling others to join in. Until one threw a stone, the rickshaw wallah paid no atten-tion. Then he yelled and flailed his arms and they bowled on faster, past a drift of water-hyacinths, heart-breaking blue, where knobbly-backed cream buffalo stood in water shaded by cream pampas grass. Behind, fields flowed to the hor-izon, brilliant with fluorescent green of rice and yellow mustard flowers. The fields were threaded with strings of people, like beads – orange and sea-green and sky-blue dots with baskets on their heads and carrying grasses. The coloured dots grew into nearer people standing by the road, the men often holding hands. Brothers helped sisters, babies carried each other along. Dogs with hard faces and dirty bristles lolled under oil drums which were houses, and a rat ran like a wicked thought from the inside of a tilted stage-coach.

'A coach! A stage coach – it can't be!'

The boy laughed.

'Time of horses. Broken.'

'But, it's a coach. A coach. It's History.'

The ridiculousness of a stage-coach among the unchanging buffalo, the medieval people, the gypsy plastic rickshaw and her own elegant, alien European figure in the midst of it made her joyful, and she smiled down at the jogging crowd of children that now accompanied her on either side, several clinging to her footplates and a long string of them out behind. She thought for the first time of the nuns' unhappiness at leaving this country.

Then they were in the village.

The rickshaw boy got off the tricycle and helped her down and they were beside a high cement wall growing out of the mud and deep puddles. The rickshaw boy looked round and seized a large child and treated it to an intense description of what would happen to it if the rickshaw were touched or breathed upon in the owner's absence. Then, bowing and bending to Venetia, he led her to a gap in the wall and down a little alley bounded by bamboo houses on stilts, flanked by tipping bamboo latrines. White hoods with holes for eyes looked down out of purdahed windows and from every door the children poured – huge bellied, gummy eyed, dirty, cheerful. Venetia saw two with chicken pox, one lying blotchy with measles. In Africa, she thought, we'd have had somewhere to take them. What had the Sisters been about? Then she thought, perhaps when the Sisters were here, there was. She looked about for the Hospice.

Children were pouring behind her now like a river, trampling on the bamboo wall of a house whose owner had laid it out upon the ground to darn. The owner, an ancient skeleton of perhaps forty in loin cloth and white, pointed beard, waved a silver scimitar at the children and his beard shook with wrath. He let Venetia pass as though invisible.

'Here now,' said the rickshaw wallah in triumph. 'The Sisters Lasadam. Jesuschrist,' and Venetia saw a tin shack with a cross nailed to the wire frame door. Through the wire there seemed to be a great many people.

'My family,' said the rickshaw wallah. 'I am Sham Su. This is Sham Su's family.'

'But this is the mission house – the Hospice.'

'Now closed,' said Sham Su. 'Here is wife and second wife. For second wife I have now found time. Here are many children of Sham Su. Here is mother of my wife and of my second wife.'

Hosts of dark eyes looked at tall Venetia. The mothers of the wives were fat, with brooding faces. They looked at Venetia's trousers with dislike and pulled their black veils tight across the nose and mouth. The wives had at once covered their faces likewise as Sham Su approached and turned away their heads. They looked very quickly at Venetia. The new wife sat in a cushiony heap, her head hanging down. Only the children crowded round unblushing.

'Please – come in,' said Sham Su. 'Here is my son.'

On a boarded table-top of trestles pushed against a wall there was a plastic mesh meat-cover. Above it on the wall was a shiny torn picture of Jesus stretching his arms out across a group of children with different coloured faces, a roseate Galilee behind. On the table, beside the meat-cover was an envelope with the Mission stamp on it, and under the mesh of the meat-cover there was a tea-towel saying Irish Linen. Apart from these, and the cross on the door, there was no indication of the forty-year mission of the Last Adam.

'My son,' said Sham Su, pointing at the meat cover, and a wife, covering her face tightly, turning her head from Venetia, came and tweaked the meat-cover away revealing beneath the tea-towel a long-lidded, long-armed frog. As Venetia looked, the frog spread its arms wide on each side and opened its mouth in a triangular yawn. The skinny arms ended in fists the size of walnuts and the walnuts opened into stars. Picasso had pencilled long black lines along the upper lids and past them. The child, scraps of bone and skin and hair, stretched all its limbs at once to the sweaty air and the eyes opened a slit and a glitter of black beneath each long lid seemed to fix Venetia and rest on her.

She moved towards the child but there was a sort of rustle in the hut, an anxiety, so she dropped her arms and only said, 'Oh, Sham Su, he is beautiful.' Silence fell among the women and the only sound was the children outside in the filthy alley calling and shouting. One of the women, sitting on the floor, passed Venetia a piece of apple she had been peeling with a bit of rusty knife-blade, and another brought a can of fizzy drink with a grey straw sticking out, its top used and flattened. In Africa, brisk, professional Venetia would have rejected all these dangerous things with confidence enough to cause no offence. Here, she accepted them, eating the thumb-marked apple slowly and drinking the drink to the end. Looking in her bag, she pushed money under the baby's head while the women bent into their veils and Sham Su looked out into the street for a moment of abstract thought. Then a child covered in sores came sidling in and put a hand on Venetia's knee. The sores were bleeding. It looked at her with wonder and she touched its cheek.

'What is left here of the Sisters?'

'The Hospice. It is for us.'

'Sham Su – I'm afraid it's not possible.'

'Yes. The Sisters say very good. No one will want. Sister Agnes knows. She helped the boy be born. All is very good.'

'The Hospice belongs –'

But the future of the shack had already been discussed, no doubt, in Calcutta. Whatever had been decided would take many months to describe and implement here. Who owned it was not Venetia's problem.

'Is there nothing left here? No furniture?'

'Nothing,' said Sham Su, smiling, 'all gone away. The Sisters are good. There is only the picture and the paper.'

'What is the paper?'

Venetia picked it up and found inside some faint notes looking very unlike accounts – just one or two pages folded into old folds. She took this, touched the frog through the tea-cloth, bowed to the women and followed Sham Su back to the rickshaw, children still streaming behind, and the rickshaw bounced again past the rag pickers and the buffalo and the hyacinths. At the railway line she said, 'Sham Su – do you miss the Sisters?'

Over his shoulder he laughed, 'Oh yes – Sisters?'

'Did they make you Christians?'

'Oh no – Muslims. All Muslims. No Christians.'

'Did they teach you?'

'Yes. English. And Jesuschrist, Son of God.'

He smiled the smile of a man with a job, where there are few, with a son who would one day support two mothers, of a man who can afford two wives and who in several years would move into a Muslim heaven. In the meantime he drove the queer, rich stranger who believed in Jesus Christ and the good Sisters about the streets and people admired him. Venetia watched the cheerful twisting way he moved his body about, the happiness of his face and his voice greeting people, his cleverness in manoevring the rickshaw through the terrifying traffic; his grace and urgent life.

'You are strong, Sham Su.'

'Yes. Very strong. Are you married, lady?'

'No.'

'I am sorry. Are you alone?'

'No – I work like the Sisters.'

'Not like Sisters' clothes?'

'No.'

'I am sorry. And no children also like Sisters?'

'No.'

His face, open to her like the children's showed pity and pleasure in her, and not a trace of desire.

He said (she gave him dollars – twice what he asked and he bowed briefly), 'I will call you auntie. Tomorrow I will bring you flowers.'

*

In the afternoon she lay on a long blue chair in the Intercontinental Hotel gardens. She took off the bright pink kaftan she had been given by the mission in Africa and lay in her bikini. 'I am forty-two,' she thought, 'and I look older. But I can still wear a bikini. Better than anyone here,' she thought, looking round at the patient, waiting wives. 'Mountains of flesh,' she thought. The men were mostly airline pilots resting. 'All fat and flab,' she thought, 'except this muscly old boy alongside sliding his eyes sideways at me under the lids.'

'Like the baby,' she thought. She pulled up her bangles – stretched her legs. 'I have good legs anyway. I have put a bangle round one of them like the Muslim women. How Mother Clare would laugh at that,' and she took out the envelope she had found in the hut.

It was no more than old notes and scraps, mostly prayers – Sister Agnes's meditations left behind. Very scant. No accounts. She let it fall, then picked it up again as the crows swooped down for it from the pergola overhead. She read again and saw that the last entry was more recent, the ink black and new. 'Bless,' it said, 'the son of Sham Su, born –' and the date of a week before. Then was written, 'Sham Su's son is born today, my last child, the last Adam. "The first Adam was made a living soul; the last Adam was made a quickening spirit."'

*

I shall be kind to the old man, Venetia thought, having dinner with him that evening and when he asked her to have a drink with him in his room afterwards, she went with him. 'I shall be kind to him,' she thought. 'It's not as if he's dangerous. He's old. He looks as if he's not got long, poor thing,' and she stood at his window looking out at the great stretch of lights across the city and far away to the river. Over the river the lights were orange pins of torches. Closer in the electric lights flickered white, more uncertain. The single, boastful Coca Cola advertisement kept going out.

'All the little alleys,' she thought. 'Maze upon maze. All the children and the sick and the old, all packed in the mud tunnels. The crowds would still be drifting round the railway line, the flares on the boxes lighting up the oranges in pyramids in the dark. The old man with the scimitar would be lying on the floor of his hut asleep, with his white beard in the air. And Sham Su in bed with his wife. Or both his wives. However did it work? ('Did they make you Christian, Sham Su?' 'No – Muslim, Muslim.') and she turned away to the funny old man, rummaging in the back of a drawer for whisky.

'Is that your wife?' she asked of a photograph.

'A long time ago.'

'You have been married a long time?'

'Thirty years.'

'Thirty years. To the same woman.'

'Perhaps,' he said. 'You'd like tea?' and held up some schoolboyish machine he had for making tea in hotel bedrooms. With his work all spread out behind him on the extra bed (like a second wife, she thought) and pride of possession in his face, he looked like Sham Su. 'If he were to ask to take me to bed –' she thought, astonishingly.

But the moment passed.

A mosquito whined about. She wondered how it got there, seven floors up. How it survived. Would the frog child survive? Half of them did not. Did it greatly matter? Rallying all her forces from the training of years, she repeated obediently, 'Thou fool, that which thou soweth is not quickened except it die.'

She thought of her sketch of a life. There had been little peace in it. One radiant time in Florence, she remembered before her attempt at the convent. She had shared a room with a girl from college, about to do Medicine – a nice sensible girl. She'd be a solid general practitioner now with a doctor husband and two wholesome children. Venetia remembered shadowy carved angels looking down at the two of them from the ceiling of the old pensione as they lay in their beds talking about the future. She could not now remember the girl's name. This was before the leaving of the convent, the years in Rome, the years of breakdown, the slow climb back up the cliff again in kindly, dotty Oxford.

'What a haphazard mess,' she thought. 'There's none of us really begun.'

But then she seemed to see the three nuns sitting side by side in the jumbo-jet – Mother Clare staring calmly ahead, Sister Agnes upright and weary with *Lord of the Flies*, Sister Ambrosine sunk in sleep and missing the dawn as it rose rainily over Zurich. Three confident people, she thought. She saw the baby stretch its skinny arms, the black glitter of its living eyes – the beloved of Sister Agnes, the last Adam, the quickening spirit.

An Unknown Child first appeared in *Vogue*
The Pig Boy first appeared in *Good Housekeeping*
A Seaside Garden first appeared in *Woman's Journal*
The Pursuit of Miss Bell first appeared in *Woman's Journal*.

BILGEWATER
Jane Gardam

Shortlisted for the Booker Prize
Winner of the Whitbread Award and David Higham and
Winifred Holtby Prizes

'Superbly told . . . adolescent anguish has no better friend than
this poignant ode to its hopes and fears.'
Times Educational Supplement

'The best of all her novels. It is funny, beautifully constructed,
deeply moving, and I cannot get it out of my mind.'
Daily Telegraph

'Jane Gardam has a deep, intuitive sympathy for victims of this
age group . . . not without an equally sharp comic appreciation
of their plight. Lively . . . excellent.' *The Times*

'A very good book indeed, witty, enriching, and a pleasure to
read.' *The Listener*

'One of the funniest, most entertaining, most unusual stories
about young love.' *Standard*

0 349 11402 1
GENERAL FICTION

BLACK FACES, WHITE FACES

Jane Gardam

This gentle, perceptive and witty collection of connecting short stories has won both the Winifred Holtby Prize and the David Higham Prize for Fiction.

'Very impressive' *Sunday Telegraph*

'A little gem' *Daily Mail*

'Gentle, funny and full of good observation' *Daily Telegraph*

'A new writer of talent and originality' *Auberon Waugh*

'Very good indeed' *Times Literary Supplement*

0 349 11407 2
FICTION

Abacus now offers an exciting range of quality fiction and non-fiction by both established and new authors. All of the books in this series are available from good bookshops, or can be ordered from the following address:

Sphere Books
Cash Sales Department
P.O. Box 11
Falmouth
Cornwall TR10 9EN.

Please send cheque or postal order (no currency), and allow 60p for postage and packing for the first book plus 25p for the second book and 15p for each additional book ordered up to a maximum charge of £1.90 in U.K.

B.F.P.O. customers please allow 60p for the first book, 25p for the second book plus 15p per copy for the next 7 books, thereafter 9p per book.

Overseas customers, including Eire, please allow £1.25 for postage and packing for the first book, 75p for the second book and 28p for each subsequent title ordered.